Volume One

AIRSHIP 27 PRODUCTIONS

The Moon Man Vol. 1

Editor: Ron Fortier
Associate Editor: Charles Saunders
Production and design by Rob Davis

Published by
Airship 27 Productions
www.airship27.com
www.airship27hangar.com

ISBN-13: 978-0615608983
ISBN-10: 0615608981

Printed in the United States of America

10 9 8 7 6 5 4 3 2 1

MOON MAN TABLE OF CONTENTS

BAIT TRAP...5
BY GARY LOVISI
Inspector McEwen comes up with a foolproof plan to capture the Moon Man which seems like curtains for the Robin Hood of Crime.

THE FALSE GLOBE..31
BY ERWIN K. ROBERTS
A phony Moon Man is terrorizing the streets of Great City and it's up to Steve Thatcher to stop this imposter before his own efforts are destroyed.

FIRE AND GLASS...71
BY KEN JANSSENS
An arsonist is on the loose in Great City and Steve Thatcher's college friend is the number one suspect. Only the Moon Man can prove him innocent.

BLACK MOON...114
BY ANDREW SALMON
The Moon Man is caught between the police and a trigger happy mercenary force.

OUT OF BUSINESS...157
BY GARY LOVISI
When Ned gets thrown in the slammer, it's up to the Moon Man to take on a mob boss solo and save his best friend and ally.

THE ROBIN HOOD OF THE PULPS................171
Afterword on the character's history by Ron Fortier

BAIT TRAP
By
Gary Lovisi

*P*olice Chief Peter Thatcher was old but regarded as a tough crime fighter throughout Great City, now he was angry because he and his small department had been getting mounting pressure to capture the most notorious criminal of them all, the mysterious Moon Man. The wily criminal had run a one-man crime wave throughout the city for more than a year now. That is why the Chief was holding this meeting today in his office. Present were ace detective Lieutenants Gilbert McEwan, Mark Keanan, and his son, Sergeant Steve Thatcher.

No one in that room knew that Steve Thatcher held a terrible secret that could place him in prison for life, because Steve Thatcher was, in fact, the notorious Moon Man!

"So how do we catch this criminal menace?" Chief Thatcher asked his men, looking for some suggestions. These were the men he trusted most and who actually ran his department. Tough cops and ace crime fighters all.

"By damn, I've tried everything, Chief," Gil McEwan spoke up quickly, allowing his frustration to show as he thought back on all the various schemes and traps he had devised over the last year, none of which had worked. He had been trying to catch this elusive criminal for months now with no success and many in the department said he had become obsessed with capturing the hated Moon Man. It was a dangerous obsessive drive that made an ace cop appear erratic and even dangerous to some. They had tried so many things that he was almost becoming suspicious that the wily criminal's escapes might be from an inside job or a leak in the department, but he knew that could never be. "The man is uncanny, but I will bring him down one day, I promise you all, and on that day he will get what he deserves."

The other men in that room all seemed to feel the same way and nodded their heads in agreement; even McEwan's best friend, Steve Thatcher.

The Moon Man was wanted for dozens of burglaries and robberies, but also for three murders, so the death penalty was involved should he ever be captured. No one but Thatcher knew that the Moon Man was innocent of those murders, however now there was no way for him to prove that innocence. Steve Thatcher accepted the situation, he knew that part of that went with the territory. As the Moon Man, his sole reason for committing his various crimes was for one reason and one reason only, he could not stand to see the suffering of the poor during these grim Depression years. So Steve donned his night black costume and with an Argus globe covering his head to obscure his identity, he became the dread hunted criminal known as the Moon Man, robbing from the rich to help those in need.

However, this criminal hunted by all was in reality a type of modern-day Robin Hood, but he did not have the support of the people because no one knew he was the person behind all the good that his criminal deeds accomplished. Instead another man, one of his agents, got that credit. Meanwhile, the police, politicians and the newspapers saw the Moon Man as a menace to society and they wanted his head. They saw him as dangerous and violent, a criminal who had killed once before and probably would kill again. They all demanded he be caught and given the electric chair.

"Well we can try to set another trap," Mark Keanan offered, he was a bulldog dick who had risen high in the department and was almost as obsessive in his hunt for the Moon Man as was Gil McEwan.

"We've tried that many times and it has never worked," Steve Thatcher said, hoping to direct the conversation away from the Moon Man to some other subject. Steve knew he had to be careful, the police had the Moon Man's thumbprint on file, taken from a door knob of one of his early burglaries, so he could be held for murder if he was ever suspected and some bright cop saw to it that he was printed.

Steve Thatcher's main problem was that Gil McEwan was his best friend and a good cop who he respected as much as he loved his own father – though McEwan's hatred for Steve's alter ego kept him forever on guard and nervous should it ever be found out that he was the Moon Man. Making Steve's life even more complicated, was that his fiancée was Sue McEwan, Gil's lovely daughter. Only Sue, and Steve's friend and associate, the ex-pug Ned Dargan, aka "Angel" knew the true identity of the Moon Man.

"Yes, a trap, I'll give it another try but only if we can get the proper plan," Chief Thatcher suggested. "It has to be something new and something that will trap this criminal. We need to get him caught in box that he can not escape."

"I don't know about that. I have to agree with Steve," Mark Keanan said showing his own frustration now. "How many times have we tried to catch this guy, only to see him slip through our fingers?"

"Too many times, by damn!" Gil McEwan growled in anger, "but I will never rest until I have brought the Moon Man to justice. Some day I will find out just who this Moon Man really is – he can't hide from me forever! Then I will catch him and make sure he ends up in the proper place for all his crimes, a nice comfy seat upon the electric chair!"

"If we can only discover his true identity," Mark Keanan mused.

"Once I discover that bit of information, it will be all over for him. I don't care who it might be; anyone in this town, even you Mark, the Chief, or even you, my best friend, Steve. I don't care who it might be," McEwan said tersely giving each man in that room a determined glare. He surely did not suspect any of them, but the tough cop was just trying to make a point. He would make no exceptions or conditions on getting the Moon Man a one-way ticket to death row. "I swear on all I hold dear that I will make sure the man pays for his crimes with his life, no matter who he might be."

"Well, we all want him captured," Steve Thatcher offered calmly. He was trying not to rile his friend up any more or to appear too askance at his friend's hateful obsession which made him nervous. "So far, though, nothing has worked."

"Yes, that's true. We have come so close on so many occasions, but then lost him always seemingly at the last minute," Chief Thatcher added, scratching his head in thought.

"But we know he craves cash," Gil McEwan told them, and as he said those words the spark of an idea formed in his tough cop brain. A plan soon came to him. It seemed to offer and chance, not only to catch the Moon Man, but to regain some of the respect he felt he had lost among his colleagues by not being able to catch this elusive criminal. Could this be the plan that trapped the Moon Man once and for all?

"Well, what is it, Gil?" Steve Thatcher asked his friend, careful not to appear too eager to discover just what was on McEwan's mind. Steve knew his friend held a relentless determination to catch the Moon man, but if Steve could find out Gil's plan here and now before it went into effect, it might save a lot of trouble later on.

"By damn, I do have a plan, something I'm thinking over," Gil McEwan told them with cagey enthusiasm, but careful not to speak too much before he had it fully formulated. It wasn't that he didn't trust the men in that room. No, not at all. In fact, he had known each of these men for many years, and he trusted each one of them with his very life. But McEwan could be such a hard-headed detective he sometimes struck out on his own, without letting anyone know what he was doing. That's what had made McEwan so successful as a detective, and that's what Steve Thatcher knew made his best friend so dangerous to him and the Moon Man.

"Come on, tell us what your plan is, Gil." Mark Keanan asked curiously. He was hot to know. "We'd all like to hear it."

"Yes, and we'll help you with it if we can," Steve Thatcher added.

Gil McEwan just shook his head, "By damn, I think I'm going to go this one alone, gentlemen. I have the germ of an idea and I want to see if it works. If so, then I'll let you all in on it later."

Soon after that the meeting broke up. No one could get Gil McEwan to disclose his plan for trapping the Moon Man and Steve Thatcher knew he would have to keep alert, and watch sharp!

The Van Arsdale mansion was the ancestral home to one of the most wealthy families in Great City. It was also the home of a family that owned most of the property in town, especially the small homes across from Murder River that were to be foreclosed on since the residents could not meet their next mortgage payment or rent. It meant that families, working men, women and mothers, and so many children would be all thrown out upon the cold city streets and this outraged the Moon Man.

As the Moon Man, Steve's every crime was committed with the express purpose of gaining as large amounts of cash as possible, which he used to help the sick and poor. He never profited by any of his crimes. In fact, he went through life a hunted and haunted man, for should his true identity ever be discovered it would not only mean a death sentence for him, but the discovery would probably kill his poor old father the police chief, devastate his best friend Gil McEwan, and destroy the love of his life, his fiancée, Sue. Sue was also the only daughter of Gil McEwan. So Steve Thatcher had a lot to consider as he drove his roadster out to the Van Arsdale mansion to meet Simon Van Arsdale.

Van Arsdale was on his way home from the city after picking up rent and mortgage payments for the buildings he and his family owned. It was said to be a tidy sum. Steve figured, that being a wealthy man from a wealthy family, Van Arsdale would not need all that cash as much as the poor and sick would be in need. So the Moon Man would pay him a visit and relieve the wealthy young man of that burden.

The road was dark and winding, large trees on either side formed mysterious shadows in the moonlight as the sleek roadster flew down the road towards its goal. It was a perfect night, and a perfect crime for the Moon Man to do his work.

Steve Thatcher finally reached the Van Arsdale mansion, parked his vehicle off a side road and then took the case out of the secret compartment of his trunk. He knew that he had to work fast, for he had only bare minutes to get dressed and into position before Simon Van Arsdale returned home.

It would be just enough time for what he planned.

Quickly and without a sound, Steve Thatcher police detective, opened the case and took out the long black robe and black gloves and put them on. They made of him an all-obscuring figure of darkness, except for his head. For the moment his face and identity were visible. He was terribly vulnerable. But not for long. For one moment later he carefully took out the two rounded hemispheres of silver from their case that were specially made to fit securely over his head. They clamped together making a perfect silver globe of glass. This Argus glass sphere entirely covered Steve's features so that no one could look into it to see his face, but Steve could see out of it clearly and breathe from it as well.

The overall effect of this dark costume was eerie and mysterious. Steve Thatcher took a quick look into the sky, knowing the moon's rays glinting off the large Argus globe over his head gave off just enough light to show a visual image that scared the daylights out of anyone who saw him.

"No wonder they call me the Moon Man," Steve whispered to himself as he took out his automatic and quickly ran the hundred yards to the front door of the Van Arsdale home.

The Moon Man quietly positioned himself behind some leafy bushes just as a large touring car pulled up the driveway and parked. There was a single occupant, Simon Van Arsdale, newly returned from the city. The young man slowly exited the vehicle. In his hand he held a black leather briefcase that was known to be filled with cash from rental and mortgage payments. That money would help the poor and sick in the city when Steve handed it over to his trusted associate, Angel, to distribute to the needy. Steve knew that the people who had paid Van Arsdale the cash in that briefcase would be credited with their payments, so that stealing this cash would not hurt them, but it could be used to help those who could not pay their rent or mortgage. Steve knew the money would go a long way to helping the small homeowners who lived along Murder River so they could keep their homes, at least for a few more months. This was Steve's sole reason for his life of crime. That is why he felt that he must continue to steal from the rich of Great City, so that he could obtain cash to help the sick and poor who were in such dire need.

"Hands up!" a mysterious voice demanded harshly.

Simon Van Arsdale froze at the sound of that menacing voice behind him. It was eerie and hollow and filled him with fear.

"Turn around!" the voice barked.

Simon Van Arsdale nervously turned to look upon the man who spoke those words, and then his fear grew to an alarming level of terror. For standing just a few feet away from him was a man covered in all-encompassing blackness, and upon his head was a large silver globe that shone eerily in the night's moonlight. He could not make out who the man might be and he did not care at that point. It was such a strange and terrifying image. It all looked so unreal to him he could not even run away.

He knew it was the dreaded Moon Man!

Van Arsdale then saw the automatic that was trained upon him.

"Don't move and you will not get hurt. I am only here for that briefcase. Hand it over," the surreal voice spoke from inside the silver globe. Van Arsdale could not see into the sphere, he could not see who the man was or what he looked like at all.

Mechanically, as if in a trance, continuing to stare at that mysterious silver globe as if transfixed by its brightness, Simon Van Arsdale handed over the black leather briefcase to the man without resistance.

"Thank you, Mr. Van Arsdale. I am sure there are those who can use this money far better than you. Now do not move and do not call out, or I shall come back for you and teach you a lesson in obedience."

Then the Moon Man was suddenly gone, melding into the darkness of the night.

Simon Van Arsdale stood there alone shaking badly in holy terror. He could not have moved or called out even if he had wanted to just then. He just looked off in open-mouthed awe hoping the dark being with the silver-globed head was gone into the dark woods never to return. He hoped he would never see such a being ever again in his life.

"Thank you, Mr. Van Arsdale."

Steve Thatcher got to his roadster without any problem, everything had worked out perfectly, almost too easy. He quickly took off the Argus globe and his black robe and gloves, collecting them with his automatic, and placed them into his regalia case. That he zipped up and stored away in the secret compartment of the trunk of his roadster. Simon Van Arsdale's black leather briefcase he put on the passenger seat beside him as he drove away.

The entire criminal event from start to finish had taken him only three minutes, and now the Moon Man was gone, his work was done, and Steve Thatcher was on the way to meet his trusted associate, Angel.

Ned Dargan, was a stocky ex-pug, a former boxer with a cauliflower ear and no neck. He appeared to be a rough brute, but he was a man with a heart of pure gold. He was one of only two people who knew the true identity of the Moon Man and he had become a trusted associate of the notorious criminal – but Ned knew the Moon Man was no criminal, Ned saw him as a white knight and a friend to the poor.

Dargan was known to the poor and sick simply as "Angel" because he had appeared to them as nothing less than an angel, so Steve Thatcher also called him by that nom de plume, rather than use his real name for safety purposes. Angel was the Moon Man's representative, he went out and presented the poor and sick with gifts of cash so they could buy food, pay rent, or afford life-saving operations needed by members of their family. He was loved by the poor and needy. He was a devoted servant who worked proudly for Steve Thatcher and the Moon Man.

"Angel, you there?" Steve Thatcher called out softly. Thatcher had driven his roadster to a dark and drab section of town by the banks of Murder River. Murder River was so-called because of the large number of corpses found floating in it each year. It was a dumping ground for the criminals of the city, a place where they got rid of their problems. Off the river, there was a drab building that the Moon Man used as a meeting place. It was desolate and perfect for his needs.

"Yeah, Boss, I'm here," Dargan said, seemingly materializing out of the dark shadows. He never called Steve by his name, only Boss, to make sure no one ever overheard his true name being spoken; just as Steve only called him Angel. This was one way the two men protected each others secret identities.

He smiled at Steve, nodded when he saw the briefcase that he held.

"Good to see you, Angel."

"You too, Boss. So how did it go tonight?"

"Like a piece of cake," Thatcher said, handing Dargan the briefcase. "Here, Angel, take this and distribute it to those in need."

"Sure, Boss," Dargan said, taking the briefcase with a grin. Soon he was gone, lost into the darkness of the night.

Steve Thatcher got back into his roadster and drive off to pick up his fiancé, Sue McEwan for a late dinner and some dancing at the Starlight Club.

The fabulous Starlight Club was the type of place where all the local swells flocked to for a fine meal and star-studded entertainment in the best classy surroundings. Valet parking took care of Steve's roadster, then he escorted Sue McEwan into the elegant supper club.

"I'm so glad you're safe, darling," Sue confided to Steve, her arm entwined with his as they made their grand entrance into the club. They were a glowing couple, a matched pair of the perfect man and woman. Along the way to their table various diners called out to Steve or Sue, recognizing the popular couple and saying hello.

"It went well," he told Sue in a soft voice. "Angel is taking care of the disbursement now."

"That will help so many people. So many need help these days," Sue said softly.

"I think so," Steve answered hopefully. He had led a privileged life, but he had seen what the Depression had done to the people of his city, how the bad economic times had taken jobs, taken homes, then taken away pride, leaving families with little or nothing. Sometimes not even food to eat. Something had to be done. Steve had made a decision over a year ago that he would be one of the ones who should make a difference and do something for these poor people. Sue and Angel helped him.

The couple sat down at a secluded and private corner table by the far wall. It was their special table. Drinks were brought over. A singer crooned a melody of lost love on the stage up front as couples got up to dance. Steve and Sue remained at their table, they only had eyes for each other.

"I'm worried, Steve," Sue finally said, taking a sip of wine and then looking into his eyes. Steve knew Sue had something on her mind about the Moon Man and that it was bothering her.

"What is it?"

"My father has it in his head to capture the Moon Man. He thinks about it night and day. You have to stay safe."

"Gil always has had it in for the Moon Man, Sue," Steve replied with a wry grin. "I fear he's obsessed."

"That's just it, Steve, I'm afraid my father won't stop until he catches you. That would be a disaster for everyone. I know he has come up with some new plan, there is something that he has been working on, and it scares me."

"Did he tell you what it is?" Steve asked hopefully. It would be good to know what Gil was up to regarding catching his alter ego. Good to evade any trap before he entered it. The cops were always setting traps for him and so far he had been able to evade capture on every one. He did not know how long he would be able to do so, certainly not forever. He feared it was just a matter of time before the Moon Man – and he – were caught.

"No, he won't talk about it, but he seems very devoted to planning it," Sue replied, her voice tinged with concern for the safety of the man that sat across the table from her – the man she loved and wanted to marry.

Just then their dinner was brought over and the two lovers ate in silence, each with their own thoughts. Sue McEwan torn between her loyalty to her father and her lover, Steve. Steve torn between his mission to help the poor as the Moon Man and what it would mean to all those closest to him – his father, his best friend, Gil, and his fiancée, Sue – should it ever be proved that he was the Moon Man. He did not care so much about himself if he were ever found out for his crimes but knew it would crush those three people – the three people he cared about most in his life.

After dinner Steve and Sue shared a couple of drinks, then rounded out the evening by dancing to a couple of numbers by the fine house dance band. After that Steve took Sue home.

It was late now, but not that late. As Steve pulled his roadster up to the McEwan house he noticed Gil standing on the front porch smoking his ever-present cigar. Steve got a bad feeling about this. It looked as though Gil was not waiting for Sue to come home at all – but for him!

Steve and Sue kissed goodnight. Then Sue got out of the car and walked towards the house, giving her father a gentle peck of a kiss as she passed him on the porch, then she slipped into the house. Steve watched her go with a deep sigh. She certainly was a vision to look at, even from behind. Then he noticed her father.

Gil McEwan did not follow his daughter into the house but continued to stand on the front porch smoking his cigar.

"Steve?" Gil called out before he could drive away. "Come on up here for a minute, I want to talk to you."

Steve Thatcher got out of his roadster, warily walking up the flower-bordered pathway toward the front porch of the McEwan house.

"Hi, Gil, out late tonight. Eh? Sue and I were just having a late supper. They have this new torch singer at the Starlight Club that's just tops," Steve told his friend with a smile. In fact, tonight's late date had been arranged by Steve and Sue partly as a cover for him should there be any embarrassing questions asked as to his whereabouts during the Simon Van Arsdale robbery.

"Did you hear about the big robbery?" Gil McEwan asked him bluntly, angry. "The Moon Man has struck again!"

"No, what happened?"

"By damn, Simon Van Arsdale himself was taken by the Moon Man right in front of his own home earlier this evening! He had a briefcase full of money that was with him," Gil told his friend. "The Moon Man took it!

"That's bad news," Steve answered showing what he hoped was proper concern as he wondered how to play this latest news.

"By damn, it is too bad, but once I get my hands on the Moon Man it will be all over for him. I promise you that."

"Well, I hope you catch him soon, Gil," Steve offered, trying to show some enthusiasm, "the man's a real menace. Once he's captured and in prison the entire city will be safer for everyone."

"By damn, Steve, not in prison! I'll see to it he gets the electric chair," Gil growled sternly.

"I see," Steve replied carefully.

"But that's not why I asked to talk to you, Steve, it being so late in the evening. I been thinking. You know I've been working on a plan, something to trap the Moon Man?"

"Yes, you mentioned it at the meeting yesterday but when I asked you what it was you kept mum," Steve stated, knowing that he had to tread carefully now.

"By damn, I was thinking of another trap."

"Not another trap?"

"Yes, but it's not what you think," McEwan said, and he showed a glint in his eye and wry grin that unsettled Steve more than any of his hard cop words ever could.

"Well, are you sure you want to tell me about it, Gil?"

"Yes, Steve, you're the only person that I will tell. I know I can trust you," Gil said with a smile now. Gil put out his cigar and then patted Steve on the shoulder in a friendly manner. "I'm gonna catch him, Steve! Here's how I plan to do it."

Steve nodded, listening intently as Gil outlined his plan. It was a decent plan, and it would have certainly drawn the attention of the Moon Man if Gil had not been telling it just then to the very man who was the Moon Man. But the knowledge now also put Steve in a delicate situation. He was now the only person who knew Gil's plan, so the Moon Man would be forced to take the bait and go into the trap, if he did not it would tip Steve's hand and that would bring suspicion to him.

"By damn, do you see the simplicity of it? We'll make it known in the newspapers that a large amount of cash is going to be picked up from the Associated Insurance Company building out on Main Street. I've already set it up with the office manager there. They have recently sold some big money policies and will have more than $50,000 in cash in their office. The bank will send an armored truck to pick up the cash. The company office and bank security are too tight for the Moon Man to attempt anything then, but the weakest link is where I am sure he will strike, just before the cash is picked up by the armored car. That will be eight o'clock at night when the armored car arrives. The papers will even post the timetable for the pick up."

"I see," Steve muttered grimly, working it over in his mind.

Gil continued, "That's the logical point when the Moon Man will strike and that's when I'll nab him! Like I say, we'll play it up big in the papers, so there will be no way he will be able to resist going for it. What do you think, Steve?"

Steve Thatcher hid a worried look and patted his friend upon the back, "Gil, I think it's a great idea, a stroke of genius. The Moon Man will never be able to resist all that cash."

"That's what I figure too, but I didn't tell you the kicker in the plan. They'll be no cash for him to get. At the last moment, the real bags will be replaced by only washers and bundles of cut paper made to look like bills. So there will be no money in the sacks for him."

"So no cash?" Steve asked, trying to hide his disappointment and the worry he felt that he hoped did not show on his face.

"No, not one penny, by damn!" Gil told him proudly. "The real cash will be put in other sacks and placed in the office safe, then picked up by an armored car the next day."

Now Steve could feel the trap closing because he knew the Moon Man could never be seen to resist such bait. If there had been cash there, Steve might even have dared the trap to get at that money. Now it was more complicated. There was cash but if it was placed into the safe he could never get at it in time.

Steve had to think this out. If he did the heist he could not go directly for the bags in the safe, he had no time to crack a safe in any case, but going for what was in the safe would also tip off Gil that the Moon Man knew the plan.

Unless the Moon Man hits them before the bags go into the safe! Steve thought that was the way to go, but he knew that was deadly dangerous to attempt. The timing had to be precise.

In fact, the way the plan had been explained to him by Gil, even making a try would be suicide. Much too dangerous. However, if the Moon Man did not attempt such an obvious heist, that would also raise questions and suspicions in Gil's mind – maybe even pointing to Steve himself. For Gil had told Steve he was the only person who knew about the plan. Gil had not even told his own daughter. Steve sighed deeply, why, oh why, had Gil even told him about this!

Steve knew that Gil certainly never suspected he could be the Moon Man, but if the ace criminal did not make an attempt for such a load of cash – thereby putting himself in jeopardy of the trap – it could lead Gil to suspicions regarding Steve he did not want made. It was a devilish situation to be in.

"The Moon Man will not be able to resist the bait, Steve," Gil told him confidently. "Then, by damn, I'll have him!"

"I don't know, Gil, the plan sounds good but..." Steve mused carefully, hiding his concern and trying to find a way to dissuade him if he could, "but you just told me the Moon Man stole a briefcase full of cash from Simon Van Arsdale. So maybe he doesn't need more cash right now. He could very well pass up your trap."

"No, and that's the other kicker, Steve," Gil told him all proud now. "The Van Arsdale ruse worked."

"Ruse?" Steve muttered, and suddenly felt his stomach lurch.

"By damn, it was a ruse, a bold ruse. You see, there was no money in that briefcase!"

"No money?" Steve asked softly, alarm quietly coursing through his body. Steve had not thought to actually open the briefcase before he gave it to Angel.

"That's right, Steve. So you see, I've finally got the Moon Man right where I want him. He's gotta be strapped for cash now, so he has no choice but to take the bait I offer. He's gotta go for it!"

Steve stood rigid, glad that Gil could not see his face in the dark night of the covered porch. "I think you're right, Gil."

"By damn, you know that I am, Steve!" McEwan said as he put out another cigar anticipating a sweet victory as he got ready to go into the house and hit he bed. "Well, that's all I wanted to tell you, Steve. So goodnight and sleep well. I just figured I'd give you this good news to cheer you up."

"You sure have, Gil," Thatcher said thoughtfully.

On the way home Steve Thatcher drove over to the building by Murder River that Ned Dargan was using as his center of operations.

"Angel?" Steve called out carefully.

From out of the darkness the stocky, ex-pug showed his face, "Yeah, Boss?"

"You all right?"

"Yeah, Boss."

"What happened with the money in the briefcase?" Steve asked.

Angel shook his head. "There was no money in the briefcase, Boss!"

"I know."

"You know, Boss? I tried to call you, I left a message at your home to call me but…

"I just found out, from Gil."

"Not good. Now what?"

"Now, I'm being forced to do a robbery for worthless bait, and it will place me in a nice little trap set by Gil McEwan."

"No, Boss, don't do it."

"I have no choice, Angel. I'm the only one Gil told his plan to, so if the Moon Man doesn't show up, suspicion will fall squarely on me."

"Then either way…?"

"Yes, Angel, it appears that either way I am cooked."

The next few days it was blared all over the city papers and on the radio news that the Associated Insurance Company had set a new record for selling insurance policies. It was a positive business story at a time when so many were out of work and business was doing badly. So it was trumpeted by all. The manager was quoted as telling the press he expected to bring in over $50,000 in cash payments. The cash would be picked up by an armored car with a police escort at precisely eight o'clock PM tomorrow after the building closed for business.

The Moon Man had other ideas. Steve Thatcher knew he had to act, the Moon Man must make an appearance, must make a try for that cash. He also knew that Gil and the boys would be waiting to spring a trap for him. But Steve had no choice. What could he do to get out of this mess? Or what could he do to turn the tables on Gil and his plan?

Once the day for the cash pick-up arrived, it turned out that the money collected was in excess of $50,000. Steve Thatcher wanted to make a play for that cash – the real cash – but he also knew that he must make a play for the fake cash first. He knew that it was bait for the Moon Man, but he had to convince everyone else that he did not know that. It was a ticklish situation. And he needed a plan as well formulated as Gil's.

Steve met with Sue and Angel for their help. The day before the robbery he told them what he wanted them to do and they reluctantly agreed. They were not reluctant because they did not want to help him, but only because they feared for his safety once they heard about the trap and realized what it could mean. Both Sue and Angel feared for Steve's capture and what it would mean.

"I'm worried, Steve," Sue had told him, he could see she was near tears.

"Me too, Boss," Angel had added softly.

"I know, but don't despair, if we keep tightly to the schedule we might pull this off. I have to take Gil's bait," he said warily, hoping these were not words that would become his epitaph.

Sue and Angel nodded reluctantly.

"Good, then we do it. Be ready! Watch sharp!"

Gil McEwan strutted through the large Associated Insurance Company building, from floor to floor, checking every area and office, then over to the manager's office on the first floor where the cash had been brought and was being counted, bundled and made ready to be placed in the company safe.

Mr. James, the finance manager was beaming, "We did very well selling these insurance policies, detective, sales from premiums are in excess of $50,000 cash."

"By damn, that's a lot, perfect bait for the Moon Man," Gil McEwan barked full of energy. "But remember, you'll not be giving those bags with the real cash to the armored car today. Instead you're to give them these, the fake bags, loaded with washers and paper wrapped up to appear to be bills."

"Sure, detective, I understand the plan. Associated wants this criminal captured as much as you do. We insure many of those who have been robbed by him. When I'm finished here I'll place the real cash bags into my office safe. There is no way your criminal will be able to crack my safe. Then tomorrow after all this is over and the Moon Man is in custody we'll secretly ship the sacks with the real cash to the bank."

"By then the Moon Man will be on his way to the electric chair," McEwan said with a wide grin.

The huge Associated Insurance Company building was loaded with cops; uniform and plainclothes detectives on patrol and stationed at key locations. One of them was Sergeant Steve Thatcher who was wondering when he would find an opportunity to act as the Moon Man.

On patrol and looking to trap Steve's alter ego were his two closest friends on the force, Lieutenants Gil McEwan and Mark Keanan. All three men, along with some uniform cops, were roving the floors and offices of the massive insurance building, now mostly empty of employees. McEwan was on patrol taking the elevator to go from floor to floor to coordinate the trap. Everything looked in readiness.

With all these police around it would be a close call, but Steve thought he saw a way to pull off the heist, if he could just have five minutes – and he knew how he could make that happen.

"We're just waiting for our pigeon to show up," Mark Keanan told Steve Thatcher, who could see his detective friend was chomping at the bit to see some action, "then Gil will spring the trap and that will be the end of the

Moon Man once and for all!"

"I certainly hope so," Thatcher said softly, allowing his confidence to show at the plan. "You really think the Moon Man will show up?"

Keanan looked at the sergeant with concern, he was getting jumpy, waiting for action. "I hope so. Steve, you think we should do a last patrol around the floors ourselves, before we get to eight o'clock and show time?"

"Sure, Mark, that sounds like a good idea," Thatcher replied with a grin. In fact, he had been waiting and hoping for just such a situation to arise so he would be free of Keanan's company. "Look, I'll take this floor and you go check the upper floor. Gil's on the first floor, so he's got things covered at the manager's office. Then we'll be all set."

"Right," Keanan said and he was off on his foot patrol.

Once Keanan was gone Steve Thatcher went into action. He quickly ran into a stairwell, down the stairs to the lower floor and opened the outside door. He let in the police officer who was standing there. It was no police officer at all, it was Angel, dressed in a police uniform and in his hands he held the regalia case containing the Moon Man's costume.

"All set, Boss?" Angel asked carefully.

"I hope so, Angel. You know, you make a convincing cop," Thatcher said with a smile, taking the case from his friend. Thatcher opened it and took out what was inside and then gave back Angel the empty case.

"No one's here, Boss?"

"They're all patrolling the upper floors, I knew the stairwells would be free. But we don't have much time."

"Then if you don't need me, I'll be off, Boss."

"We'll meet up in a few minutes."

Angel was already gone as Thatcher quickly donned the black robe, black gloves, and carefully placed the Argus globe upon his head. He grasped the automatic in his hand.

Now he had become the Moon Man!

Now he knew he was vulnerable if caught in McEwan's trap, so he had to move fast. The only saving grace was that the silver globe on his head obscured his face and identity – if no one shot it to pieces! The Argus glass was delicate; a bullet, even a fist or a wooden club could shatter it into dozens of pieces and thereby reveal Steve's face and identity. But the Moon Man must make an appearance here tonight and Steve was going to make sure he did that now.

Steve Thatcher waited nervously. He waited while Angel did his part of the plan, running to the third floor and mentioning to one of the uniform

"You make a convincing cop."

cops there that he thought he saw the Moon Man coming into the building from the roof. Steve knew that news would be quickly reported and he hoped it would draw off McEwan and his men long enough for the Moon Man to act.

Angel would not stay around long enough to be questioned, but would then meet Steve in the manager's office on the first floor. But timing was crucial, everything had to run perfectly. Sue was outside waiting. Things were coming to a head and Steve had to act now. He took a deep breath, then opened the stairwell door.

Steve walked into the first floor and carefully looked around. There was no one there. Angel's ruse had drawn off McEwan and his men, but for how long?

Steve knew he had very little time to act so he ran down the floor and quickly entered the manager's office. There he saw Mr. James and two men on his staff busy putting the finishing touches on the cash count, having already bagged the cash. The safe door was open. They were preparing to put the bags into the company safe.

He would put a stop to that now!

The three men had not heard or seen the Moon Man when he entered the outer office. They did not notice him now as he silently moved towards them. The manager and his two employees froze once they saw the strange being that stood so menacingly before them. It was a man shrouded in blackness and upon his head shone a gleaming silver globe that obscured his identity perfectly. They also noticed the automatic held in his hand that was pointed squarely at them.

"The Moon Man!" James cried in alarm.

"Do not talk! Do not make a move! Hand me the sacks of coins and cash now!"

The manager, fearing for his life, for he had heard all the dark rumors about this vile criminal – all of them being very bad – quickly did as he was told. But he had the presence of mind to do as he was told the way McEwan wanted him to do things. Steve noticed that right off, for James handed the Moon Man one of the sacks of fake coins.

Steve Thatcher smiled, the bag of washers. So far so good.

The Moon Man picked up the sack of coins, then as if losing his grip because it was so heavy, he allowed it to drop to the floor in such a manner so it would split open. It did. Out poured hundreds of useless steel washers instead of shiny silver dollar coins as should have done.

"What's this?" the Moon Man growled, waving his automatic menacingly at the three terrified men. Their ruse had been found out and they feared for their lives now. Good, that's just the impression Steve was aiming for. "Fakes! Fake money! So then it must all be fake!"

Then to verify the fact, the Moon Man quickly tore open one of the bags that contained bundles of bills and saw that they were fake as well.

"Get down! Lay on the floor!' the Moon Man commanded tersely.

Mr. James and his men lay face down upon the floor terrified for their very lives. The men remained quiet and covered their eyes. James and his men had never expected this. James had been told, actually assured by McEwan, that the Moon Man would take the bait and be gone quickly. He thought that McEwan and his men would be on duty here to catch this bold criminal. Where were they?

No one heard or saw the other man enter the manager's office.

Steve Thatcher nodded to Angel, who was still dressed in a police uniform. Steve pointed to the sacks atop the manager's desk in the back of the room. The cash had been counted and bagged and was ready and waiting to be placed into the company safe. That would not happen now. Steve smiled nodding to his accomplice.

Angel quickly picked up the two sacks that contained over $50,000 in cash, leaving the heavy bags of coins behind, then he instantly left the office. The Moon Man right behind him.

No one heard or saw Angel and the Moon Man escape. McEwan was no where in sight. The entire theft had taken less than three minutes and not one shot had been fired.

It was not yet eight o'clock.

Minutes before Gil McEwan had been making his final round to check that all was well, then he heard a report that the Moon Man had been spotted by a uniform cop coming down from the roof. This made sense, the bold criminal doing something so unexpected to enter the building. McEwan pulled all his men to the upper floor and the roof. He took an elevator to the third floor himself, hoping to quickly make the capture and arrest himself. However, nothing was found and McEwan was soon enraged. He demanded to know which uniform cop had originated the report. That cop seemed nowhere to be found.

McEwan realized he had been snookered. With the elevator in use he ran down the three flights of stairs to barge into the manager's office.

When he got there he was met by a bizarre scene. At first look it appeared to him that the entire office was empty. Where was everyone? Where was Mr. James and his two men? Then McEwan noticed the three men lying motionless and face-down on the floor in the back of the office. They were quiet but shivering in fear.

"What's going on here?" McEwan barked, drawing his gun.

James looked up from the floor, sighed in deep relief, "Is it all right now? Is he gone? Is it safe? Where were you!"

"What happened?"

"What do you think! The Moon Man was here!" James spouted in alarm and sharply indignant, getting to his feet now, along with his two employees. They were still scared and astounded by what had happened here so quickly. They were still in shock.

"The Moon Man? Here! How?" McEwan barked loudly. Then he noticed all the washers on the floor and the torn bag, he also spotted the other bag that had been ripped open with the fake bundles lying on the floor. "By damn!"

"The Moon Man came in like a ghost. He was here, then gone, in the blink of an eye," James cried. "And so was my money!"

"He didn't fall for the bait?" McEwan asked in surprise.

James sighed, "Yes, he did fall for it, he went straight for the fake bags that I gave him, but then he dropped one of the bags of coins to the floor and it burst open. That gave the game away, he saw the washers, knew it was a trap."

"He escaped?" McEwan shouted.

"That's not the worst of it, detective. The bags with the real cash in them were on my desk ready to be placed into the safe. He got to them first and took the two bags full of bills. That is over $50,000 in cash!"

"By damn!"

Just then Mark Keanan and Steve Thatcher rushed into the manager's office.

"I heard there might be trouble," Keanan asked breathing heavy. It was obvious he had been running hard.

"What happened here?" Thatcher burst in, looking around, looking angry.

"The Moon Man is what happened!" McEwan barked angrily, frustration getting the better of him. He'd been bested again! "He took the bait all right, but then one of the bags broke open. My ill luck, by damn! That gave the plan away. But the worse thing is he found the bags of real cash that were on the manager's desk and took those."

"You didn't put that money into the safe?" Steve Thatcher asked the manager sharply, trying to deflect some of the blame from his friend, Gil, to the manager where it rightly belonged. "That cash should have already been in the safe."

James looked chastened, defeated, said softly, "We didn't have time. It all happened so fast."

"By Damn!" McEwan shouted. "All right, we close down this building right now, maybe we can still catch him."

"That's right, Gil, he can't have gotten far," Thatcher added sharply in faux rage.

Gil McEwan became a whirlwind of action, shouting orders to all his men. Anyone in the building was to be held by the cops for questioning. Keanan and Thatcher were told to collect some uniform cops; Keanan to do a systematic sweep of each floor of the building, Thatcher to do a sweep outside the building and upon the nearby streets.

Ned Dargan calmly walked out of the Associated Insurance Company building through a back door stairway. He was still dressed in a police uniform. He held the Moon Man's regalia case with costume in it in one hand, in the other hand he held two sacks filled with bundles of cash.

A small roadster suddenly drove up to him with timeless precision. The passenger door was flung open and Dargan got into the roadster as it quickly drove off. It was driven by a lovely young woman who was Gil McEwan's daughter. They had been gone more than five minutes when Steve Thatcher with a handful of uniform cops finally began his sweep for the Moon Man outside the building. Needless to say, the Moon Man was never found. Nor was the cash.

"This was a fiasco, McEwan!" Chief Peter Thatcher told them all in a meeting the next day in his office in police headquarters. "The Associated Insurance Company finance manager and the owners are just livid. They thought helping us with the capture of the Moon Man would end up lowering their insurance payouts, instead they lost $50,000 in cash. Your plan backfired, McEwan!"

"Don't be so hard on Gil, Pop," Steve Thatcher said in defense of his best friend. "He had a good plan, the Moon Man took the bait but who could ever imagine that bag of washers would break open and alert him to the ruse. It was just bad luck, that's all."

"Bad luck..." Chief Thatcher blurted. "Or bad..."

"Well he got away with the cash sure enough," Mark Keanan added curious, shaking his head. "It's uncanny."

"By damn, he did, but that part is the fault of Mr. James, the finance manager," McEwan barked defensively. He'd take his dose of medicine for this mess but he wasn't going to take the fall for everything regarding this royal screw-up. Especially not the mistake made by Mr. James by leaving the bags of money sitting there out in the open. It was an invitation to the Moon Man. "James had the bags out on his desk, instead of in the safe where they belonged."

"James told me he had just finished counting and bagging the cash when the Moon Man suddenly appeared," Keanan noted.

"Damn uncanny timing. Perfect timing, I'd say," Steve Thatcher observed, inwardly smiling to himself that he was able to pull it all off with such finesse.

"By damn," McEwan barked, "what a mess I concocted!"

"The worst thing of all is that the Moon Man has escaped our clutches once again and taken $50,000 in cash with him," Chief Thatcher stated with a dark shake of his head.

"Yes, he got away again," McEwan admitted, his defeat tinged with anger.

"Well, he'll not get away so easy the next time," Steve Thatcher added, trying to buoy the spirits of his father and his two detective friends. "I'm sure it's just a matter of time before we catch the Moon Man."

Many hours later Steve Thatcher drove his roadster to a drab building in a drab part of town.

"So was it good?" Thatcher asked his friend and associate, Ned Dargan.

"Yes, Boss, real good, over $50,000 in cash, just like you said. It was a very good haul. I made the delivery to a lot of people in need. This time it will go a long way to help them to pay their rent and mortgages, so they can stay in their homes."

"Thank you, Angel," Thatcher said with a satisfied smile. If this was the final result of his crimes, if he was able to help the poor or sick through these actions, then whatever he had to go through to achieve his aims was worth it.

"And since the Moon Man took the bait, you and he escaped the trap, right, Boss?"

"For now, Angel. I escaped for now."

THE END

PHASES OF THE MOON
Part One

The Moon Man may be one of the least-likely of pulp heroes but he is certainly one of the most compelling. The Argus-domed criminal hero surely makes a strange sight as he robs from the rich to help the poor. In many ways he was a perfect figure for the Depression Era 1930s. Moon Man creator, Frederick C. Davis, was a crime and hard-boiled author of the classic pulp-era who presented adventures that were action-packed, well-plotted tales with a unique hero when our country needed him most, at a time when there was just too much poverty and despair. The stories really hit a chord with the readers back then – and may even have additional meaning today – for those of us who have been hurt by the present economic woes. Davis created a modern-day Robin Hood for the urban masses. The Moon Man had substantial hurdles to overcome in his work, one aspect of the fascination these tales held for readers back then was in the often ingenious methods he went about escaping detection as he fulfilled his mission.

The Moon Man – aka Steve Thatcher, wears the Argus globe to hide his identity from those closest to him, and to instill fear and mystery. It works. Wearing the silvery glass globe, Thatcher can see out but it is impossible for anyone to see in. In the darkness of night it is the only part of him visible, giving an eerie and terrifying vision to all who see him. Such a character can make for fascinating pulp fiction and Davis gave us many wonderful stories in his original series. So what I wanted to do, was write my two stories in this book to read as much like those original pulp tales by Davis as possible. I tried to imitate Davis' style, his language, plotting, and his characterizations. I hope I have succeeded.

In "Bait Trap" I aimed to recreate a standard Moon Man novella that would read like it came right out of a 1930s pulp, as once again various forces conspire to capture the supposed Great City master criminal, meanwhile Steve Thatcher watches in alarm as his friends and brother police officers go after his alter ego with a burning frenzy.

Gary's essay continues after the story OUT OF BUSINESS...

THE FALSE GLOBE
by
Erwin. K. Roberts

Fall 1933

*T*he La Salle roadster sat on the shoulder of the road. The sheet metal of the hood steamed lazily as the big scattered drops of drizzle hit it. Stopped on the crest of a hill, the lights of a town, an over sized village really, gleamed in the foggy valley below. On the next hilltop ahead stood a group of buildings. The moist air barely allowed the glow of the sanitarium's lighting to reach the next hill eastward. Nothing of consequence showed in the cars' back window. The far distant lights of Great City merely allowed the horizon to be differentiated from the gloomy sky.

A man dozed in the car. Careful not to make himself too comfortable, his head rested against the driver's side window. A deer bounded across the gravel surface behind the roadster. The creature's passing kicked up a small stone that ricocheted off the rumble seat cover.

Steve Thatcher woke with a start. His hand flashed to the Colt Model 1911 under his jacket. Fortunately he caught a glimpse of the deer as the animal vanished into the windbreak growth on the other side of the road.

Smiling wryly to himself he let go of the pistol. He willed his muscles to relax. Then it hit him. He had been dreaming when he woke. Steve rarely remembered his dreams. This was an exception. His dream recounted some of the last trip he took with his parents before his mother's health declined. Memories flooded back as he took stock of the situation.

People said that the little town of Folley Springs up ahead rolled up the sidewalks at six in the evening, dusk or not. True, or not, Steve intended to wait until a lot more of the town's lights were extinguished before he took the only road through the place to Dr. Tryce's facility.

Steve felt removed from the world. He smiled at some of the fragmented memories his dream sent spinning past his mind's eye. How did those wonderful days in Europe bring him to this deserted road in the middle of nowhere? Would he be on this mission if the family had simply gone to the lake as in the summers before?

Ahead Thatcher saw a patch of lights at the edge of town go out. The Armory. Drill night had ended. The part time soldiers would scatter soon. Even those who stopped at the town's two bars to get one for the road would not be long.

Doc Tryce expected him sometime tonight. Time unspecified. Tryce understood that a Detective Sergeant on the biggest police force in the region could not keep a firm schedule for a meeting that would never officially happen. Radio reports about the crisis in Great City still bounded all across the forty eight states. Tryce would be kept informed, even if he had no time to listen himself.

The wild day almost caused Thatcher to call and cancel. He needed the rest desperately. However much Steve trusted Dr. Tryce and his staff, he still had not been able to stop in and check on the Angel's condition. He owed Angel that. He owed himself, and Sue, that.

When Angel was fit, Stephen would offer him the choice to leave his association with the Moon Man. To start anew, in another city, or to continue to pass out the Moon Man's stolen money to those in most need of it. Steve sighed in the roadster. He would make the offer, but he knew the Angel's answer. The Angel believed in what he did for Steve and The Moon Man.

The Angel would never have believed the early reports that morning, no matter how hard his bell had been rung recently. No, he would not believe the reports that claimed.

Steve himself had been with his father, Police Chief Peter Thatcher when the call came. Over a very early breakfast they anticipated a rare morning together at the local country club. The elder Thatcher rose long before his housekeeper could arrive to prepare the rough and ready breakfast. Waiting for the coffee to finish perking Steve put his father's clubs in the rumble of his La Salle roadster. Making sure that a large black box disappeared behind a blanket and some emergency reflectors Steve headed back inside. He didn't even make it back to the breakfast nook.

"Get the car, Steve," called his father from where he stood phone in one hand. His other hand covered the receiver. "Report claims the Moon Man cracked the armored car carrying the Ford plant payroll. Happened up in the Wyandotte area."

As Steve headed out the door he heard enough to know that his father was throwing every available vehicle and man into a containment net around the area. The Moon Man sat at the top of the list that the Great City Police Department sought. What Chief Thatcher did not know was that the Moon Man could not possibly be the robber.

The Moon Man had an iron clad alibi. After all, the Chief himself had served the Moon Man breakfast as the robbery happened. Chief Thatcher then jumped into the Moon Man's car to inspect the scene of the Moon Man's alleged crime. The older Thatcher complimented the Moon Man's driving skills as he and the Moon Man pulled up at the scene of the crime. Chief Thatcher could testify to the Moon Man's innocence of the crime. But only if Chief Thatcher knew that his own son Steve was the Moon Man.

A patrolman that Steve did not recognize hurried forward as the uniformed Peter Thatcher climbed out of the vehicle. Older than most, he crisply saluted.

"G'morning, sir, I'm Reynolds. First on the scene with my partner Gillium. He's giving information to Lt. McEwen in the dry cleaners down the block. McEwen asked me to watch for you, or other V.I.P.'s that came along. Seems like every reporter in town got here right on the heels of a patrol car or wheel officer. Good deal that we got the area roped off first thing. Fingerprint crew is on the way. Photog, too. McEwen suggested you go to the dry cleaner's roof for a look at the whole scene."

Peter Thatcher managed a small smile. "Thank you, Reynolds. Good report. Lead the way to that roof. Didn't you just come to us from Chicago?"

"Yes, sir. Just finished the Academy when the politicians decided to cut back on hiring. I owe Great City, and you, a big thanks for taking me on. Watch your uniform. Fire escape's full of rust,"

"I remember seeing your personnel jacket now," said the Chief above the rattling of the iron steps. "You were a Military Police Corporal with the Rainbow Division during the Great War. Say, is that blood I see on your jodhpurs?"

"Probably, sir," replied Reynolds. "I had to get a tourniquet on the leg of one of the men in the armored car. They put two rounds right through the passenger side of the windshield with a Browning Automatic Rifle. Then one man kept the driver covered with the B.A.R. They popped the back end open with explosives. Shattered every bit of glass I've seen since I arrived. Crooks grabbed the cash and scrammed. Concussion flattened the two guards in the back. Flying door handle laid open one of their legs. Both were alive when the ambulance tore out of here. But, even if they live, their bells are gonna be ringing for months. The driver ended up punchy but awake. That's how we got what I just told you. Here we are. Please step over here and take a look."

Steve followed this father over the tar and gravel roof. He could see steam or smoke rising beyond the edge of the roof. First the top of the building across the street appeared beyond the façade of the dry cleaning shop's front. Then the upper floor. It's smoke, Steve decided. Noises increased. With two final steps the street below came into full view.

Steve heard a mild oath escape his father's lips. His own jaw dropped a bit as the took in the scene. The armored car, one of the newest in the city, appeared like a toy that a child had ripped apart in anger.

The vehicle hung over a wide ditch. The crumpled front grill was smashed into the far wall of the four foot deep trench. The undercarriage dragged ground at the center of the vehicle. Steve decided the round length of metal mostly hidden by loose dirt must be the drive shaft. But it was the rear area reminded him of a painting by Salvidor Dali. The back wall of the armored car's rear compartment no longer connected to the side walls. Instead the sections on either side of the door twisted up and away from the rest. For an odd moment Steve wondered if the thing was trying to sprout wings.

"Holy Mother of nightmares," whispered Peter Thatcher. He pointed across the street. Steve drew in his breath and froze. From his third floor vantage point he could see something sticking out of the second story roofing across the street. "Holy crow! Is that the door?"

Reynolds broke his silence. "That's right gentlemen. That door must weigh at least a hundred pounds. It went through the wall right between the center windows. Knocked the apartment's icebox over and stuck between two ceiling joists. Just as neat as you please."

Steve fought to get a meaningful question out of his jumbled thoughts. "What could do this? Good lord, were any civilians hurt?"

Reynolds shook his head, "We found lots of minor injuries. Cuts by flying glass. People deafened, maybe a bit shell shocked. McEwen has a couple boys getting a head count of residents. Unless somebody's heart stopped and hasn't been found, we got real lucky on the civilian side. Sorry, but I don't think I heard your name."

Before Steve could reply his father spoke up, "Reynolds, this is my son Detective Sergeant Steve Thatcher. He doesn't usually drive me around."

"Yes, sir, I know his reputation. I though it might be him. What did this, Sergeant? Only one thing I know, a shaped explosive charge. Frankly this job looks like military engineers designed it. Seems like the gang took over a water department dig. Expanded it into a vehicle trap. Add a little of what the Frenchies called camouflage. Then ka-zam, you got a lock box that has to sit there and wait for the big boom."

Steve thought for a moment as the group headed back down to the street. Finally he said, "Patrolman Reynolds it sounds to me like you have some useful background that applies here. As soon as you can arrange it I want you to gather your thoughts about the military aspects of this crime. Make notes if you have to. Then call the stenographers at headquarters. Have them transcribe what you have to say. Don't worry about grammar, just the facts. Add any theory you might have, marked as theory. The stenos will send it to me, if I don't have a chance to talk to you before I leave."

"Will do, Sergeant. Thanks for your confidence."

As they entered the rear of the dry cleaners Peter Thatcher told his son, "I'll have to go face the reporters very soon. Find out where the investigation stands. Fill me in while you drive me to headquarters."

Gil McEwen greeted his Chief with a grim smile. "Chief, we're getting a lot of information, but no real leads. At least so far. Someone fitting the general description of the Moon Man led the raid. But there were four or five others. On top of that, the main ditch that trapped the armored car was dug by real city employees. A witness knew a couple of them. Public Works is finding 'em for us."

The older Thatcher nodded, "Anything to identify the gang members.?"

"No sir," replied McEwen. "Seems everybody gawked at the Moon Man. The rest wore bandannas and big hats."

"Very well. Fill Steve in. I'll go face the fourth estate." With that, the Great City Chief of Police headed for the door.

Knowing full well that the Moon Man was not involved Steve Thatcher wondered why McEwen had not launched into one of tirades about catching the notorious criminal. "Why did you say 'general description' about the Moon Man?"

McEwen stepped away from the two civilians in the room. Quietly he said, "Steve, I like to think I know the Moon Man better than anybody. Much as I'd like this to be another nail in his coffin, the job doesn't really fit him. He usually works alone, 'cept for that Angel character. Fights his own battles. He almost never shows up in the daytime. The topper is that he looked different. The big cloak he wears hides his movements. What he pulls out can be a big surprise, believe me. This time he had a holster belt with all kinds of stuff on it. But all that could be window dressing. One thing's always been the same. The blessed thing he wears on his head. Always a perfect mirror. Never a flaw seen, until today. Two witnesses say that parts of the globe didn't seem near as shiny as the rest. Parts where he'd look out. If this is the Moon Man, he's dragging more red herrings past us than we'd find at Freeman's Kosher Deli. Or somebody else is."

Steve brightened a bit at McEwen's reply. Sometimes the departments best man catcher didn't think too straight with the Moon Man involved. "If this is a phony Moon Man, I'd bet on an out of town operation," Steve said forcefully.

"Right you are son," came the reply. "Not many local lads have the gall to put him after them."

As he drove his father towards downtown Steve told his father, "I think McEwen's right. This job just doesn't fit the Moon Man."

"Then I'm glad I quoted his use of the term 'general description,' Steve. If he didn't do this, the real Moon Man won't take this lying down. Not by a long shot. I'll tell Lt. Dunning that you are assigned to the case. You've proved yourself far too often for anyone to question such an assignment from me. Go your own way if you need to, but help McEwen break this quickly!"

Steve and his father parted ways in the garage at headquarters. Steve hurried to the phone room. He read the carbon copies of all the phone messages taken related to the case. Then he buttonholed two members of the Robbery Detail. He asked them about safe blowers and other crooks that might use explosives. He did the same for one senior detective who specialized in bank jobs.

Steve borrowed the Desk Sergeant's phone before he headed up to what would surely be near chaos around his desk. Paging through a small note book he asked the operator for a number down in Great City's Union Station area.

"Yard Security, Sanderson speaking."

"Phil, this is Steve Thatcher. Sorry, I'm in a rush, but have you heard about the armored car job this morning?"

"Sure have, Steve," drawled Sanderson, the head railroad bull for the common track area of the city. "You being in a rush is no surprise.

Something we can do for you?"

Steve paused for a moment to collect his thoughts. "Maybe so, Phil. Somebody used a bunch of explosives. Opened the back of the armored car like you'd open a can of corned beef hash with lumberjack's double bitted ax. There's no obviously missing explosives here in town. We're canvasing all the known legal users, of course, but the charges might have been shipped in. Now me, I sure would not want to truck explosives over the public highways around here, if I didn't have to. Would you? Even if you didn't work for the railroads?"

"That's for sure, Steve," chuckled Sanderson. "I don't think we have knowingly moved any unusual amounts of explosives through the yards."

"Now I'm not surprised," sighed Steve. "This job was too well planned for that. I'd like you and your boys to ask around about anything strange for the last month or so. You know, people overly concerned about what should be a routine shipment. It might be one big crate, or several smaller things."

"I'll look into it," Sanderson replied. "Any nervous Nelly's or hulking bodyguards for a shipment of wine glasses, and you'll hear from me. Good luck Steve. Sounds like you'll need it."

Steve headed up to the steno pool. As he waited for the last two pages of Officer Reynolds' report to clatter out of a typewriter he composed a telegram on a pad of blanks found on nearly every desk in Headquarters.

When the Moon Man first burst on the scene the St. Louis Clarion sent a senior reporter to cover the story. He and Steve hit it off. One evening they sat in the back room of a quiet restaurant sipping bootleg beer. They debated whether repeal of Prohibition could happen before 1934 began.

Later the topic came back to the Moon Man. "Steve," asked the newspaperman, "have you heard of the fellow in England referred to as The Saint? No? Not surprising. He's not getting much ink on this side of the Atlantic. Not yet. Over there my brethren call him 'The Robin Hood of Modern Crime.' He steals from what he calls 'the ungodly,' then gives most of the proceeds to charity. This Moon Man seems to have similar ideas. For some reason the Clarion chain's home office takes a serious interest in mysterious folks like him. And on both sides of the law. If you ever need information about these figures of mystery wire me at my paper. I'll make sure you get anything we have."

Steve collected Reynolds' report from the steno. He dropped the first copy in the fast growing master case file in McEwen's work area. He kept one onion skin copy for himself. Quickly he exited the building in the direction of City Hall. After stretching his legs for two blocks Steve stepped into a small Western Union office. He handed the telegram form over to the operator.

"Sergeant," croaked the man as he pulled down his reading glasses, "I wish you'd take a course in penmanship."

"Sorry, Ron," replied Steve. "Any reply could be important."

"Let me read it back to you then. 'St. Louis Clarion. Attention Kennedy. Armored car job here. (stop) Need similar jobs other places. (stop) Factors: military precision possible military engineer background. (stop) Shaped charge explosives. (stop) 3 to 10 men. (stop) Leader dressed as local figure or highly recognizable character. (stop-signed) S. Thatcher Great City PD.'"

As soon as he returned Steve circulated all over the headquarters building. He made notes. He passed information to several harried offices and laboratory technicians. All the while he tried to digest the myriad of facts into a single theory about the blatant attack on the peace of the city. Over an hour later he gave his father a briefing. By then the Seth Thomas clock on the office wall showed a few minutes past noon. "If you don't need me, dad," he said, "I'll get some lunch."

Sue McEwen's face showed disappointment as she stepped out of the lunch counter a block over from headquarters. Her eyes bounded up from the sidewalk as someone told her, "You shouldn't be looking down, gorgeous! People will be disappointed not seeing your beautiful eyes."

"Steve!" The word popped out of her as she almost jumped into his arms. She clung to his neck after they kissed, whispering, "I was so worried about you. Afraid you'd go charging off looking for the 'Moon Man.'"

Thatcher smiled grimly, "If I knew where to charge, I'd be doing it, sweetheart. I can't let this go unanswered. One way, or another."

"Do you have any idea at all, Steve?"

"Do you remember me saying that I had a pigeon I've been saving for a rainy day? You do... Well, even though the sun is out with not a cloud in the sky, today is that rainy day. Let's get some lunch, then I'll tell you about it."

His dream this time covered that wonderful day he spent with the Forester. He accompanied the man on his rounds through Sherwood Forest. A frame in his home still held the dried leaves he collected that day from the mighty Sherwood Oak. After that evening's meal his father called

"I was worried about you."

him into the study of the home where they lodged. There stood an English gentleman with a quiet twinkle in his eye. "Good evening, Stephen," said the man. "I'm told you would like to meet me. I am Abraham Parkes, the Sheriff of Nottingham." Steve woke with a start.

Steve's arms still felt leaden as he stretched them around the passenger space of the roadster. Glad of even the short nap, he looked around the isolated hilltop. Not much to see, he concluded, with virtually no light. He thought back to that lunch with Sue. Except for coffee and a Baby Ruth candy bar that hash house's blue plate special represented his last meal.

He smiled at the thought of Sue's company. How much she helped him. Just having her to talk to about his life as the Moon Man meant so much. But that was far from all the help she gave.

When he asked how the bruises on her arm were doing her eyes flashed. Then she put on the barest hint of a smile. Her hand quickly covered his mouth, stifling any further words.

"Steve, please." Her voice was barely audible amid the sounds of the lunch counter. "I never want you to bring the subject up again. There is no need. I can see how much it hurts you. Please promise me, never again. Don't mention it. Don't think about it. I'm fine. I'll be fine."

In the tiny restaurant Steve felt shocked at Sue's firmness and finality. Sitting in that isolated roadster he felt tears well up in his eyes. Tears of gratitude. Tears of wonder at Sue's strength and loyalty. This wonderful girl wanted to be, no, demanded to be his partner in everything. Still.

As the Moon Man, his own hands put those bruises in her. Her father held the Angel hostage, hidden in a secret place. She allowed the Moon Man to torture her in front of her father to reveal the Angel's location. Her arm ended up with bloody welts around it. Calling out his real name would have ended her pain. She played along until her own father caved in. The first time they were alone after that horrible incident Steve begged her to forgive him. She managed a smile as she told him, "The Angel is my friend, too, Steve. There is nothing to forgive." Now she had closed the subject with such a finality that his heart eased. She still wanted him. She still wanted to help him.

Steve smiled in the roadster. He leaned his head back against the window to try to doze off again. The events after that wonderful lunch were part of the reason he was so tired.

Myron Glyck was ready to relax. Another two minutes and the monthly worry would be over. Myron Glyck did not realize his worries, for the week, for the month, and possibly for a number of years were just beginning.

Every month Glick took Marty The Banker lunch at the man's office in downtown Great City. Sometimes Myron chuckled, sometimes he worried, about the location being just a couple of blocks from City Hall. Not to mention about the same distance from Police Headquarters. Myron carried a brown paper bag. He always brought one. Last month the bag came from Wong's Chop Suey parlor. Today it was full of tamales wrapped in what Myron thought might be corn husks. For some reason Marty really liked all this foreign stuff. Well, the food wasn't the important part of the bag. Folded in with the paper napkins were several one hundred dollar bills.

Marty sure was big. He had to be to even pretend to eat some of all the food delivered to his office. Somebody brought in breakfast at eight o'clock sharp when Marty The Banker's bodyguard opened the office door for business. At 10:30 somebody else brought donuts and coffee. Somebody like Myron turned up at noon with lunch. More coffee and something came in at three. Myron had no idea who might drop off dinner when the office closed, but he knew it happened. Once in a while Glyck wondered if Marty even had a kitchen in that big old house of his out on the edge of town. Not that he needed one. With all the cash coming in with five drops a day, six days a week he could afford to have the best places in town send stuff there. Must be nice, thought Myron as he opened the door to Marty's "Investment" office.

By one way glass Marty The Banker watched his body guards pass little Myron Glyck into his office. Glyck played the food game well. Some dumb bag men brought the same thing every time. Like clock work. Glyck actually had the nerve to ask what The Banker would like. "I'll try about anything that don't have raw meat in it," Marty told him. "So long as the place's got a decent rep." So when Glyck brought in the union money to be invested, lunch was usually a surprise. Marty had no idea how big a surprise this meal would contain.

Myron Glyck entered the banker's sanctum. With only a brief greeting he handed over the official envelope. This contained the "on the books" deposit. Marty The Banker carefully logged the deposit into the ledger. Gave Myron a hand written receipt on embossed paper. The twice counted cash he handed to his "Book Keeper" named Laurence, better known as Larry the Lug. Larry ever so carefully placed the deposit and a carbon copy of the deposit slip in the main safe under the watchful eye of the two other office workers. Every transition was as precise as the last. Nobody, not the best District Attorney, or any other shyster lawyer could break their recollections about "public money."

Back in the office Marty asked Glyck, "So what's for lunch?"

Myron enjoyed this part. He unpacked the big bag as its flavorful smells drifted around the room. "Some guys told me this Mex with a push cart had good stuff. Hope you like the things. Sign on the cart calls 'em Tae-Mails, only with a what-you-call-it apostrophe at the end." He spread the stuff on the tray by the side of the banker's desk.

Marty sniffed the air, not sure if he'd like the things or not. Worth a try he said to himself. Then he followed the unvarying script and told Myron, "Put those paper napkins in the closet. I'll use my cloth one today. Think I'll need it."

Marty watched Glyck open the door to place the "off the books" cash on the closet shelf. He could testify that he had never seen the cash in any bagman's hands and speak the truth. All the bag men knew that the money would be counted and verified later. And everything better match up. Or else. Suddenly he realized that Myron Glyck stood frozen with the closet door half open. The door blocked his view, but he could tell that the bagman's face seemed white as a sheet. Marty drew in breath to yell for the boys when the door slammed open.

Myron Glyck staggered back against the desk. He started to move his hands. Quickly he thought better of it. Only then did Marty The Banker see the figure as it took a couple of steps out of the closet. A shapeless black cloak draped the apparition from shoulder to heel. One hand extended through a narrow silt in the thing. That hand held a big automatic pistol. Looked like the military model the former Doughboys liked so much. The snout of the piece pointed square between Marty and Myron.

Marty looked up where the face should be. His own miniature face looked back at him, all bent and stuff. Instead of a head, a perfect sphere sat firmly atop the shoulders. A perfect sphere that was also a perfect mirror. Marty mouthed three words, "The Moon Man."

A muffled voice came from behind that mirror. A voice that meant serious business. "Don't move, or else!"

Neither man moved as the black figure with the shining head strode quickly to the office door. He reached the door just as Larry the Lug barged through. Larry paused as he saw his boss unhurt and the visitor not in a threatening posture. Then he glimpsed something moving toward him from the side. A split second later the butt of the Colt Model 1911 automatic pistol made some minor indentations in his scalp. The Lug became a lump on the floor.

A moment later the pistol roared once. Marty heard a strangled groan from Dillon, the official guard. A single word came from behind the globe of glass. "DON'T!"

Lefty, the last man in the outer office, apparently didn't. The globe spoke again, "He's only creased. Lock the outside door. Then haul him in here."

Dillon's face contorted with pain as Lefty helped him into the office. They passed just out of reach of the Moon Man. Suddenly Dillon's face widened as his eyes focused on the Argus glass globe. "Ya' looked different at Samir's," he said through clenched teeth.

The Moon Man closed and locked the door behind them. "Settle down," he told the group. "Marty here is just going to make a charitable contribution. The cops may show up here because of that shot. I'll bet one of you shot his buddy while cleaning your gun. I'm not going to touch your above board money. There's no robbery if nothing is stolen. I am going to clean out your closet Marty. That will help a bunch of people on hard times.

"You will come looking for me. Look all you want. But there is an impostor in town. Watch out! He's got lots of help." With that, the Moon Man's other hand emerged from the cloak to pick up the phone. "Police headquarters," he told the operator. "Headquarters? This is a concerned citizen. I just saw the Moon Man in the Walltower Building. On the third floor. Where is he now? I got one look at that shiny head of his and ducked into an empty office. Grabbed a phone. Don't know if he's still here."

With that the Moon Man hung up the phone and backed into the closet. As he pulled the heavy metal door closed he said, "I know all about your emergency tunnel, Marty. And how to block it. This money will do a lot of good. Just beware of false Moon Men."

Five minutes later Steve Thatcher carried two bags up a set of outside basement stairs two blocks over from Marty The Banker's office. One bag contained the whole contents of Marty's closet. That could be sorted later. The other sack held the box that protected the precious Argus glass globe and the other regalia of the Moon Man. The outlaw's heavy autoloader rested there, as well. He now carried his official .38 caliber police issue revolver. Steve himself wore painter's coveralls with glasses and a few splotches of paint on his skin for good measure. He walked a block to where a painter's truck waited. As soon as he climbed in the passenger's side the vehicle smoothly slipped into gear and pulled away from the curve.

Steve looked over at the other painter who drove. Even with the painter's cap pulled low the beauty of Sue's features could not be hidden from Steve. He reached over and gently pulled one hand from the steering wheel. He kissed the hand. "Thank you, sweetheart," he told her.

Back on the isolated hilltop Steve chuckled at what happened next. Her lovely hand slipped out of his like a greased eel. It flashed into the wad of paint rags she'd been cleaning her hands with when he slid into the seat. A voice deeper than he'd ever heard Sue produce before filled the cab of the truck. A real Warner Brothers gangster accent told him, "Watch it, copper! Or yose'll get it where it really hurts..." The beautiful small hand held a hammerless .32 automatic pistol pointed where no man ever wanted any weapon aimed.

Steve would have given a lot to know just what his face looked like at that point. A moment later Sue's normal voice told him, "Don't be afraid darling. The safety is on. I'd probably chip a nail getting it off in a hurry. And I'd only do that if I really intended to shoot."

Steve laughed again as a brief shower pinged across the sheet metal of the roadster. He'd parted company with Sue a short time later.

He returned the paint truck and thanked the owner for its use in an undercover operation. With the two bags transferred to the rumble of the La Salle, Steve retrieved a small sack of change from under the driver's seat. He stopped at the first outdoor pay telephone he saw. He made call after call seeking information.

Sanderson, the yard bull, reported one possibly suspect cargo. There had been some confusion about the number of crates containing a pipe organ. One document listed 32 packing cases. The official rail line manifest totaled 37. That, in itself, did not raise any eyebrows. What followed did.

As soon as the new owner of said organ heard about the discrepancy, things happened. Lots of things. Telegrams began showing up on an hourly basis. First they came from senior officials of the rail line itself. Then a congressman sent one in. Local government officials called the freight office directly. Sanderson told Steve that the poor yardmaster seemed resigned to a direct visit from the All Mighty Himself at any time.

Just after dawn the following morning a sensible explanation emerged. The pipe organ was not intended for a church. It was a refugee from the "Talkies." A major motion picture theater in Chicago decided that it no longer needed an organ with hundreds of real and false pipes taking up space that could be used for seating. Out it went during a major renovation. Somebody in Great City bought the thing, extra sound effects equipment, and all. Packaged for shipping, the monstrous contraption filled over a boxcar and a half. A special crew, hired to take the organ apart, then install it in Great City, included their tools and equipment with the shipment. That caused the confusion. The installation would be complete by the end of next week at a private residence.

Steve rolled his eyes as he spoke into the phone. Only one family, the highest flake in the upper crust of Great City, coveted music enough to fit this story. And the patriarch of the clan felt so far superior to the common man that he tolerated not a bit of delay from anybody. "Oh ho," he told the yard bull, "this could only be the Yardley clan at work. Correct?"

"Correct, Steve. Boy, am I glad that mess is over. If this helps you out, tread lightly. Old man Yardley was ready to chew nails and spit tacks over the deal."

"I'll leave your name out of it," Steve said with a smile. Then he hummed the first few bars of the song 'Happy Days Are Here Again...' Finally he said, "Thanks, pal, but please don't stop listening for me."

Steve's next call ended when he reached his father's secretary. His father faced the press yet again. "Molly, I want any idea you can give me if dad stays tied up. I need to go out to the Yardley estate. One possible armored car clue leads to some people working temporarily there. I better find someone to grease the skids for me, or everyone from the Mayor to J. Edgar Hoover will have the vapors when I reach the front gate."

His calls finished, Steve drove to one of the roughest parts of town. He pulled into a Cities Service gas station at the edge of the Lowrey Hill neighborhood. Owned by a long retired cop, Steve knew his car would be undisturbed there. After pleasantries with the owner, he caught a bus to ride the four blocks to his destination.

At the corner of Alger and Beadle streets Steve exited the bus quickly. He ducked into the Alger entrance of a Rexall drug store and out the Beadle street door. Six quick steps and he climbed a flight of stairs. He banged loudly on the door at the top. He held his shield and ID card next to his face.

A moment later he heard a low pop as a loud speaker warmed up. Finally a voice asked, "You got a warrant, officer?"

Steve grinned as he put his identification away. It was not a pleasant grin. "If I have to get a warrant to talk to the staff of this 'private club' it will be served on the end of a battering ram by a dozen of the biggest cops on the force. Behind them will be the federal, state, and local liquor control boys. Right now it's in your best interest to talk to me. And by that I don't mean I've got my hand out."

Steve could hear the mike go "dead" for a brief time, then it hummed back to life with the message, "Be there in just a minute." In just about that time the door eased open.

"Come in. Sergeant Thatcher, isn't it?" The voice was smooth. The face was not. The double breasted, pin-striped, suit was of excellent hand tailored quality and fit. Samier's face looked like it spent time in a concrete mixer, regularly.

Samier's worked hard at being a step above the average establishment on "the other side of the street" from what Steve represented. The true riff-raff, the hop-heads, and especially suspected stool pigeons never came through that door. Or so the stories said. If the gin came from somebody's bathtub, then the tub's owner knew exactly what he was doing. Or so the stories said.

A few of the faces nursing a drink, or having a late lunch in the main area, were familiar to Steve. Anybody wanted by so much as the dog catcher would be tucked away. Steve halted in the middle of the common area. Quietly he told Samier, "Thank you, Samier. We'll speak in a moment. I want to talk to the whole house."

He turned as he spoke to those at the tables and at the bar. "I am Detective Sergeant Steve Thatcher. I'm working the armored car case. If you haven't heard about that job, then you must be in the wrong place. Or I am." That got a grudging chuckle out of most of them. "Witnesses say the leader dressed like the Moon Man. I say 'dressed like' for a reason. Some folks are wondering if it really was the Moon Man.

"Then, I get this call. Out of the blue. This fellow claims the Moon Man showed up here. Now I know he didn't stop in for Samier's fine food. Not with that thing on his head. Not for a drink, either. Not without a real long straw." Several faces held amused looks now. They expected to be threatened, not entertained.

Steve continued in a lower voice. "That caller I mentioned claimed to

"Come in. Sergeant Thatcher, isn't it?"

be the Moon Man. 'The real one' he said. Says he's got a witness he can turn over to me to prove that a Moon Man was here. If and when that makes it to the public record Samier will be tied up in red tape until the cows come home... on the next fourth of July. Everybody ever suspected of being in here even once will be a witness. Since the money in the armored car still belonged to a federally chartered bank, the feds could send Elliot Ness's best buddies to take a hand.

"You can talk to me, off the record, in Samier's office, or while I walk around. Turn a deaf ear to me, then I got to report that call. That, and I'll bet you the real Moon Man jumps in with both feet, somehow. Think about it. I'll be around."

Steve walked down the steps from the "private club" about an hour later. During that time, information had come. Mostly in tiny bits and pieces. He stood everywhere. He looked out every window in the place. He listened. He paused at the bar and ordered a sarsaparilla. That they didn't have, so he settled for a ginger ale. And he listened. He took close looks at every painting and picture in the place. He listened some more. He shone his tiny penlight on the oddball chandelier. And kept his ears perked up amid chuckles from some customers. He even visited the restroom. After that he returned to the bar to chase the ginger ale with a shot of milk. That they had. Seemed Samier ate shredded wheat for breakfast. Finally, he chatted with Samier in the man's office. Phone calls frequently came in for Samier. From within the club.

A word at a time. A quick phrase. A line at a time. A short verbal image here and there. He stood at a window. A voice at a near table grew briefly louder. A very quiet word from the man at a bar stool when he picked up his drink. Messages relayed by Samier in the office. Information flowed to him.

Nothing official. Not a bit could stand up in court. In fact, the District Attorney would have a horse laugh at how he obtained the story of what happened at Samier's five days before the robbery.

Somebody from out of town bought an introduction to the club. That cost serious money. It also required at least two "in" people at vouch for the newcomer. The fellow showed up at the appointed time with the right words and token. A bulky man he was with hair and beard right out of a Sherlock Holmes story. Once inside he asked to use the restroom. It was the Moon Man in cloak and globe that emerged from that facility. This "Moon Man" wanted to recruit some good hands for a one time operation. Meet him at such and such times and places to apply. He thanked one and all, then took his departure in a waiting sedan.

That concluded the main narrative. The whispers and asides told much more. "Went to the second place. He didn't show." "You've seen him," said a fellow while Steve waited for his milk. "The thing on his head was smooth as the best shootin' marble ever made, right? Thought so. This guy's what you call it was flat in the front. 'Bout where he'd look out." "Got the idea he didn't care who showed up at the meets." "Moon Man's supposed to be near average size. This one's six one, maybe six two."

Steve arrived back at headquarters about three o'clock. He found McEwen studying the now heavy case file. "Sit down, Steve," he called. "I gather you've been running in all directions. Take a load off."

Steve plopped down in the suspect's chair at McEwen's paper covered desk. "I've got lines in the water everywhere. Even my lunch with Sue turned out to be more about work than anything else. She can see the forest when I'm too busy looking at individual trees. That's a big help sometimes. By the way, she says to remind you to eat and drink on a regular basis."

"She would," chuckled McEwen wryly. "Say, thanks for putting Patrolman Reynolds' report in the file. Read it. Got Rogers and Phillips checking the Armories for information on blasting experts. Probably nothing there, but we got to cover it."

"You're leaning toward an out of town gang then?" replied Steve.

"Unless the real Moon Man's running one Hell of a blazer on us, it's got to be. I can think of a few crooks and one or two 'respectable' people in town that might attempt something this big. But even three sheets to the wind on bad bathtub gin, not one of them would have the gall to get the Moon Man after 'em. Do you agree, my boy?"

Steve pulled out the notes he made at the garage before driving back to headquarters. "Indeed I do..."

His report finished, Steve headed for his father's office. Peter Thatcher stood with the door the tiny private restroom open. He used the mirror on that door to readjust his uniform to its usual precise look.

Since nobody could hear what was said, Steve could not resist a verbal jab. "'S matter, Dad," he drawled? "His Honor try to take a chunk out of your bottom?"

The elder Thatcher harrumphed. "He hasn't had time to be mad at me. Not yet. He's talked to Henry Ford himself at least three times today. With Ford's financial backing His Honor's staff is scrambling to assemble enough cash to pay the factory workers at the end of the shift in a few hours. And we have got to protect that delivery. I've a meeting on that in twenty minutes."

"This team might make a second try, at that. I'm just glad this didn't happen during FDR's 'bank holiday' last March," said Steve.

"Saints preserve us, no. I don't even want to think about that," the Chief replied as he finished rebuttoning his jacket. "Molly gave me your message. Old man Yardley has delusions of Godhood. Fortunately, just this once, I've got him over a barrel. Did you know that we still haven't closed the books on the Annual Policeman's Ball last month? Beyond the terrible loss of our brothers in the heist itself, that robbery upset a lot of things. Like a number of very well to do people Brandon Yardley shows up at the Ball just long enough to present a letter of credit. Then takes a bow for his generosity. Just between us the old boy is like the Pharisee in the parable about giving. Gives of his excess, but he does give.

"Anywhere he was there, about to have his picture taken, when all Hell broke loose. His bodyguard hauled him out quickly. So we never received the donation promised in his letter. Yardley gets upset at a lot, but I think he hates a welcher more that just about anything. He'll also do about anything to avoid being seen as one. I'll tell him that we held off bothering him about his well publicized donation until we had a need to send someone to his digs on business. There may be whiffs of smoke coming out of his collar, but he'll be polite and cooperative."

Steve smiled as he drove the the last few miles to the huge Yardley compound. The fall leaves were at their zenith. Full afternoon sun caused them to positively pulse with color in the gentle breeze. He let the driving mostly take care of itself as he allowed his mind free rein on the case, or away from it.

Of all things, the front gate turned out to have a drawbridge. Steve pulled up to the outer gate house. It looked about the same size and shape of an English Police Call Box. A uniformed armed attendant stepped out. Steve rolled the window down the last turn. He flipped open the folder that held his badge and identification. "I am Detective Sergeant Steve Thatcher. I'm expected."

"Yes you are, sir. I'll have them lower the entry for you," said the guard politely. He turned and signaled the larger box across the gap.

Steve watched the end of the bridge carefully as it lowered. The underside seemed very damp. Moss and slime clung to quite a bit of it. With his mouth not seeming to move Steve said, "And you raised the thing just to impress the visiting Copper?"

"Of course, sir," the man told Steve with a wink. "The gate on the other side will stop anything this side of a war tank. Enjoy your visit. When the drive branches follow the side with the Greek statuary to the parking area."

Steve thanked him and rolled across the heavy iron and wood bridge. He parked the La Salle and surveyed the scene. Mansion? Check. Lavish French garden maze? Check. Small outdoor amphitheater cum orchestra bowl? Check. But what in the name of Boulder Dam was behind that sixty foot tall circular black curtain?

A bright female laugh from the wide lawn startled him. "Ugly, isn't it?"

Steve turned to find that the thick lawn had muffled the approach of a vibrant woman astride a pure white Arabian horse. As he watched her energetic dismount Steve found himself attracted to her in spite of himself. As she approached Steve realized that her well proportioned body was at least three inches taller than his. She was far from plain. She was not quite beautiful. She was one of a kind. A kind that naturally attracted men. And she knew it.

She glanced at his credentials briefly. "Sergeant Thatcher, I'm Maria Yardley. Let's get my Uncle's part of this done. Then everyone can stop walking on eggshells and relax a bit. Please follow me."

Maria's riding outfit was not overly tight, but Steve could quickly tell that she had a ballerina's body with not a bit of fat to be found. She led the way to the main house. They entered by what Steve decided had to be the tradesman's entrance. A long series of nearly bare corridors led to the master of the manse's office.

As a young teenager Steve's Boy Scout Troop held a winter survival overnight at the ruins of Fort Ripley, near Little Falls, Minnesota. In their improvised shelters they huddled together through a thirty-two degree below zero night. As he followed Maria Yardley back into the afternoon sun Steve decided he had felt warmer that night in Minnesota. He stretched his whole body for a moment as he let the sun pour down on his face.

Maria's deep laugh still managed to sound very feminine. She smiled at Steve saying, "Let me guess. You won't want ice in a drink for a week?"

Steve mumbled something about being glad to have the bank draft in his coat pocket.

"Very diplomatic of you, Sergeant," she said lightly. "Now who was it that you needed to speak to?"

"The people putting in that monster of an organ your family bought," replied Steve.

"Follow me," she said with a smile as she led him towards the tall black curtain. "Uncle Brandon hates a work in progress, but he walks in the garden every day. Since he couldn't just stay away from the construction area he decided to hide it."

They passed through a heavy black canvas tunnel. Steve paused as he saw a rolling hillside half converted into terraces. A new marble structure almost abutted the orchestra bowl. Maria headed inside.

"I fell in love with that theater organ while I studied at the Sherwood Conservatory of Music in Chicago," continued Maria as she guided Steve around stacked up seating. "Now it will be mine to play. The whole west end of the building opens up. When we entertain I can serenade over two hundred on the terraces. Ahhh, those legs sticking out from under the pipes must be Mr. Eisenhower, the head installer."

The little man quickly extracted himself. Maria introduced Steve.

"One moment please, Sergeant," said Eisenhower. "I must test this latest adjustment." His hand quickly ran up and down a two octave scale. Aside from hearing the notes, Steve felt them in the soles of his shoes and every tooth in his mouth.

As the pipe sounds faded he heard Maria sigh, "Oh, that is so very much better, Mr. E. Wonderful! Sergeant, I'll leave you to your business. Head back to the garden when you are done."

"Would you like to see my credentials, Mr. Eisenhower?"

"No need, my friend," he replied. "If you are not Houdini himself, the Yardleys will have made sure of you. Ask your questions, but I have no idea how I could help you."

"Well, sir, there was some confusion at the rail yards about your shipment of tools."

"Not my tools. Their tools."

Steve blinked, "I think we'd better back up a bit. Who are 'they'?"

"Of course, Sergeant. I am a Master Tuner of keyboard instruments. That is in the old usage. I brought with me only my nephew, who is my Apprentice. Soon to be Journeyman, I think. We are all that is required to make this instrument play as it should. My contract also required, wisely so, that I supervise the disassembly in Chicago, and the rebuilding here.

"When the news of the project became public many wanted to do the work. Not surprising, in these times. One group of six men, all cousins they said, made an unusual offer. They would do the job for room, board, and help in relocating to Great City where work waited for them with another family member. Fortunately I had two grand piano installations to do. They required abilities similar to this project. I paid them to do these as a test. They worked with great speed, skill, and respect to all they encountered. The Yardleys' agent approved them.

"I had two boxcars entirely reserved for the organ. Far more than needed. The men arrived with four heavy packing cases said to contain all their worldly goods and a fifth with what they needed for the job. They completed their part of the work flawlessly in just over three days. The estate's staff trucked them and their crates into town. My nephew and I continue the much longer task of tuning. Maria Yardley is a fine musician, with a better ear than most. We are far from finished."

Steve copied the information on the men gathered for Income Tax purposes. By then Eisenhower was back at work. Steve loudly thanked his feet before he left.

As Maria walked Steve back to the parking area he saw at least a dozen men identically dressed in gold and blue now raking leaves, trimming bushes, and generally sprucing things up. "Where did this crew pop up from?"

"They're from a service. My Aunt arm twisted Uncle Brandon to host a little gathering tonight."

Back in town Steve stopped in at the Great City Gazette building. Winking at the retired cop working the lobby he climbed two flights of stairs to the features area. Compared to the bustling city room the place seemed like a library. His quarry stood at a big layout table marking the full sized mock-up pages with blue and red pencil.

"So you're looking for experts in explosives, aren't you?"

"Of course we are," replied Steve. Given Roberts' knowledge of the region, anything might be coming. "McEwen has good men talking to people at the quarries, the State road builders, and even the National Guard Armories. Off the record, the gang might have someone with a military background."

"Could be. Could be the whole gang served together Over There. Remember, a lot of companies, battalions, and even some much bigger units got formed out of youngsters from the same general areas. That all Colored regiment, for one. The Hellfighters from Harlem, the Frenchies called 'em. Came mostly from the New York City area.

"Tell me Steve, how many Doughboys came home and tried to make a go of it, legit. Then come these truly hard times. Suppose you, and all your buddies, get the rug pulled out from under you. And you've done nothing wrong. A group of pals who grew up together, trained and fought together, might decide to get even with the world together. Ever thought about that?"

"Much as McEwen, and my father, hate the idea we are considering the possibility," said Steve. "Anything else you have for me, Erwin?"

"Just one more item, Steve. Did you know that one of the most famous safe and vault blowers is in town?"

"You're kidding," exclaimed Steve coming half out of his chair!

"Easy, Steve. He's not involved. At least not directly. Arvin "Snaps" Salinger has been up the river for the last ten years. I got word last week he got called to testify at the trial of a former cell mate. If he isn't at the State Court building, he'll be a guest of the county."

Grabbing his hat, Steve rose. "Thanks, Erwin. Say, why do they call him Snaps?"

"Because when he blew a safe the sound was supposed to be no louder than a finger snap. Very skilled man according to the paper's morgue. Make your calls from the desk by the door. Good luck, Steve."

Soon Steve hurried over to the county lockup. There he met Salinger, a man of about sixty years. He looked bored, but brightened at the chance to talk about his trade. "Sergeant, there are usually three types of folks who use explosives on my side of the fence. Least that's the way it was in Chicago 'fore I moved up here. First are the idiot amateurs. A lot of the old time train robbers were that way. The Hole In The Wall Gang vaporized more cash than they got away with. Then there's the protection guys and one or two killers for hire. They don't have to have much skill. They don't care how much material they use long as the job gets done. Then there's pros like me. We work as small and quiet as we can. We measure explosive by the dram and drop, not by the stick. Whether you care, or not, guys like me take pride in our work being safe. Helps us get away undetected, you know.

"From what you say, this group didn't learn their trade on my side of the street. Sure sounds like they knew what they were doing. I played around with shaped charges a time or two. That's damn tricky. Sometimes you even have to melt the actual explosive. Not many have both the brains and the nerve for that. No reports of big amounts of missing explosives locally? Then they either have legit access to a large supply locally, or they shipped it in. Probably by rail. I'd be damn careful if you corner them. With their kind of bravado they might try anything."

Before returning to headquarters Steve stopped at a sidewalk newsstand that doubled as a private message drop for him. The three foot ten inch owner gave him the high sign as the La Salle rolled up. He asked for a Baby Ruth bar as an all clear signal. He paid for the candy and a copy of the Gazette, then rolled on. He found a telegram slipped in with the funny pages. It read, "Mr. Smith wants meeting. Urgent." The signature stood for Dr. Tryce. The Angel wanted to see him. And neither he nor Tryce misused the word urgent. At the next Western Union office he passed he sent a coded reply, "On way this evening. If possible."

At headquarters Steve headed up the stairs to McEwen's area. They met on the landing as McEwen came charging down. "Steve, meet me three blocks northwest of the robbery site. On Grant off of Holmes. One of our search teams found explosives," he called in passing.

Steve dashed upstairs. He scribbled a quick summery of his trip to the Yardley estate. He dropped the report in the case file as he hurried out to the communications center. There he told the supervisor, "Find Patrolman Reynolds. Have him report to Grant and Holmes with lights and siren, if necessary." With that he headed back to his La Salle, glad he'd topped off the tank earlier in the day.

Steve took every shortcut he knew getting to Grant and Holmes. Back alleys with lots of missing cobblestones rattled his teeth. He dodged around the car barriers on a buses only bridge that saved him half a mile. Two near misses and a tight squeeze later he arrived.

Down the block he saw McEwen's unmarked vehicle, a patrol car and a pair of police Indian motorcycles. A patrolman stood twenty yards to either side of the door where the vehicles were parked blocking the sidewalk. Steve parked at the intersection and walked toward that door. As he finished cutting across Grant Street a large Hudson sedan with Army markings pulled up. Steve greeted a tall Major and a blocky Sergeant as they alighted.

"Good afternoon, Sergeant. I'm Major Albright. This is Sergeant Simmons. Lt. McEwen asked us to stand by with our most knowledgeable demolitions man to evaluate any materials found. Simmons is up from Chicago to give our units here explosives training tomorrow night."

Steve led them inside. As his eyes adjusted to the gloom of a vacant storefront he could make out Reynolds on hands and knees peering intently at a very strange contraption that sat next to a timber crib made of railroad ties. Someone had bent a seven foot long piece of inch thick boiler plating into an eighteen inch deep "U" shape. Welded to each end were two inch thick square plates. Steve could see that the metal device would drop neatly into the crib. Additional balks of wood nearby seemed to be raisers both flat and angled. Steve started to introduce the soldiers when Simmons spoke for the first time.

"Shorty Reynolds, is that you?"

Reynolds hopped back in alarm, then burst out laughing. "Well, I'll be pickled in vinegar! Stockade Simmons, in the flesh. The Army's not given you the heave-ho yet?"

"Not hardly," chuckled Simmons. "Major, this used to be MP Corporal Reynolds. Provided security on a lot of unexploded stuff for us in France."

With that Simmons fell to examining the device. Finally he said, "Definitely intended as a 'cutting' charge. Wax cover to prevent contamination. Several precut holes in the explosive for blasting caps. Coils of wire are mounted on the timber carrier, so they fired electrically. With practice, a team could place and arm the thing in a minute, maybe a bit less. Professional job, but nothing really unusual."

Questions were asked and answered. The fingerprint and camera team arrived. Steve caught McEwen's eye to indicate his leaving. McEwen nodded. Steve moved back out into the afternoon sun. He found Reynolds waiting.

The man wasted no time. "Sergeant, something is off center here with Simmons. Either his memory is going, he needs glasses, or he's holding something back. The wire attached to the wood. That exact method was not in the American manual. I saw it taught to American teams twice by Limey Engineers. Sappers they call them. Most U.S. Engineers in the War never saw that trick.

"I don't know about Simmons today. Back in the war he always had some sort of scheme cooking. Nothing really bad or dangerous, but always trying some sort of con. I personally escorted him to the stockade twice for minor stuff. Just be aware."

Steve found a pay phone. The communications chief at headquarters came on the line as soon as he identified himself. "Telegram came in, Steve. So hot old man Fortier ran it over himself. Quoting: 'Similar jobs Pierre, South Dakota and Chicago. General Custer and Buffalo Bill Cody involved respectively. See Roberts Gazette teletype details. Kennedy.' I hope that makes sense to you."

Sense indeed. The La Salle's tires protested at the u-turn back to the storefront. Reynolds' partner had been relieved. Steve pulled up as they prepared to mount their machines. He gave terse instructions. "Reynolds, make whatever kind of excuse you have to. Spend some time with Simmons. Find out if he's been to South Dakota lately."

Reynolds frowned, "You suspect him in this, Sergeant?"

"Not really. At least not yet, but where he's been on duty, and off, might be important," Steve replied, then snapped his fingers. "'Nother thought. Find out if his trip here was a last minute deal or long planned."

"Will do, Sergeant. We haven't managed to squeeze in lunch yet. I'll ask him to join us at a place near the Armory. Its only two miles west."

"When you're done, try reaching me in the editorial area of the Great City Gazette building," Steve told the Wheel Officer as he headed out.

Back at the Gazette a private security guard escorted Steve to a small conference room in the heart of the building. Roberts waved him to a chair with his double pointed red and blue pencil. "Looks like the case's got you going in two or three directions at the same time, Steve. Anything you can tell me?"

Steve arched his back in the chair and tried to twist the kinks out of his arms. "Not much. At least not directly on the case. Can you tell me anything about the event the Yardleys are throwing tonight?"

"Until today, not much," replied Roberts. "Last week Andy Frain, the Usher King, came in with his advance party."

"Frain, and his blue and gold. That's why the grounds keeper uniforms looked familiar out there," exclaimed Steve.

"Is that so. Anyway, yesterday I got word that the senior gemologist for Tiffany's is staying down at the Plaza Hotel. Since then my spies have reported that senior people from Saks Fifth Avenue, and at least five other very exclusive retailers have arrived there with large amounts of so-called luggage. The hotel's safe is said to be bulging.

"Now, as to why you rushed in here," smiled Roberts, pulling out a roll of yellow paper out of his briefcase. "This came over the private wire right from the New York Clarion. All six feet of it. Sounds like you struck pay dirt."

Eagerly Steve began scrolling through the roll. Earlier in the year a gang had snatched a railroad car out of the Pierre yards by hijacking a switch engine. They headed out an old spur line that no road followed to an abandoned mining area. Just outside the populated area explosives destroyed three full lengths of track behind them. Leading the raid, on horseback, was General George Armstrong Custer.

Later in the year a mounted double of Buffalo Bill Cody led an attack on the Arlington Park race track at Arlington Heights, near Chicago. Just after the last race carefully prepared explosives blew a hole into the counting room. All the betting and concession receipts from 20,000 spectators disappeared down the road out as more charges dropped several utility

"Eagerly Steve began scrolling through the roll..."

poles in the path of pursuers.

Steve put down the roll. "Wow," he breathed. As he caught his mental breath the extension phone in the room buzzed. Roberts listened momentarily, then silently slid the instrument across the table.

"Thatcher."

"Sergeant, this is Reynolds. Simmons is Regular Army based out of Fort Sheridan in Chicago. He goes to a different state about every month. He was in South Dakota in March. He's worried about something, Sergeant. Got more and more nervous with every question I asked. When I asked how he got along with the Major, he about dropped a clinker. I think that... Holy S..."

Steve heard the sound of movement, followed by a loud bang with breaking glass. Then he held a dead line.

Certain the call had terminated, Steve called headquarters. He gave communications what he knew. He shoved the tele-type paper roll in his inside jacket pocket. He remembered to yell a thank you to Roberts just before the door slammed behind him. Soon he drove like a maniac in the direction of the National Guard Armory. A call became slowly audible as police radio in the dash warmed.

"...cars in the area 37th Street and Wyoming. Shooting with injuries. Officer involved. Ambulance requested. Repeat: All cars in the area 37th Street and..."

Steve had his siren on. He adjusted his destination to that of the radio call. The La Salle almost overturned once as he dodged someone pulling out of an alley. As he approached 37th Street he barely heard a siren of different pitch. Steve braked hard just before entering the intersection. It was well that he did. The heavy Paddy Wagon that usually carried the Riot Squad would have smashed the roadster otherwise. Almost on the vehicle's bumper came his father's official car. Steve fell in behind them.

With an officer reported injured Peter Thatcher usually managed to drop everything and head to the scene. Important meetings often continued in the sedan as it raced through the streets. Steve knew that more than once the first familiar face the hurt man recognized was that of his Chief.

The three vehicles squealed to a halt in front of a small drugstore. Steve sprang from the La Salle. He ducked around an ambulance, then came to quick stop as he saw Reynolds seated by the store's front door on two bundles of the Gazette's afternoon edition.

Blood from a number of minor cuts on his face and hands had dried. His uniform jacket lay in a heap at his side. His blouse had been ripped open. He leaned against the wall to hold an improvised dressing against a wound that ran down his back. He waived at the approaching men with a pained smile.

"Not to worry, Chief. Not about me, at least. I got real lucky. The doc, the orderly, and the ambulance driver, are seeing to people inside hurt worse'n me. Men from those two patrol cars are helping and checking the neighborhood."

"Charlie, get blankets and medical bag from the trunk," the Chief told his driver. "What happened here, Reynolds?"

"The pay phone's just inside the door at the end of the soda fountain. I was leaning against the wall talking to Sergeant Thatcher. Suddenly I got this feeling somebody's watching me. I look out the door and there's this Studebaker rolling to a stop with the passenger door even with me. Out the window pops the muzzle of a B.A.R. I dive and roll. The first slug of a three round burst creases my shoulder. Before the gunner can reset his sight picture I put three .38 rounds into his door. The Studie pulls away. Not sure I hit anyone."

"Where was your partner?" asked the Chief as Charlie put a heavy blanket over Reynolds.

"Lucky thing, sir. He was at the magazine rack in the back trying to find the new issue of something called Doc Savage. If he'd been with me, or outside the punks mighta' just sprayed the whole place and we'd both be dead. Instead, they tried to take me out neatly. I ducked. Short as I am, all three rounds hit the bottom of the phone box. Otherwise the poor soda jerk would probably be dead. Seems the phone company hadn't emptied the coin box in months. The coins musta stopped the first two rounds, but the third shattered the metal case. Sent coins all over the store like shrapnel. Officer Gillium ended up with a quarter embedded in his nose. Bled worse than I did. So no pursuit, sorry to say."

As he put the scene of the shooting behind him Steve collected his thoughts. The gang must have a second target he decided. Otherwise they would simply jump in a hole, put on the cover and hide until the the heat was off. And what about that device discovered near the auto plant? Could that be a red herring? Or a leftover? Everything today seemed to revolve around Chicago. Steve stopped at the nearest precinct to make some long distance calls.

An hour before dusk Steve again approached the Yardley estate. Leaving the La Salle in the empty barn of a foreclosed farm, Steve headed across the untilled fields on a wide tired bicycle. He wore threadbare dark clothing he received in trade for warm garments from a man at the Salvation Army shelter. His face appeared darkly unshaven at first glance. Strapped on his back rode a large haversack.

Five hundred yards from the Yardley property, Steve hid the bike in the bushes of a windbreak. Pulling binoculars from his pack, he scanned the estate's property line. He saw nothing out of the ordinary. Carefully he climbed the rolling hill in the direction of the drawbridge. Nothing, but that close to the gate, not unexpected.

He retraced his steps into the shallow valley to climb up the other side. He remembered the words of the old Ojibwa Indian who worked at his Boy Scout Camp. He crested the hill on hands and knees, shaking the tall grasses as little as possible. He repeated the move at the next hill crest.

It was well he did. He caught a whiff of cigarette smoke in the barest of breezes hitting his face. A wide but shallow graveled drainage ravine crossed the downslope less than fifty yards on the windward side. In it sat the brand new 1934 Studebaker Model T&W stake and platform truck. Identification photos of the new Studie had arrived at Great City PD only three weeks ago. The brand new vehicle stood facing away from the Yardley estate heavily decorated with mud. Straw poked out from under the tarp that arched up over the back.

Steve stifled a laugh as he looked at the man smoking on the running board. He wore almost the exact same clothing as the farmer in Grant Wood's controversial recent painting called American Gothic. But instead of a pitchfork, a Springfield '03 rifle leaned against the running board.

Steve slid back out of sight of the truck. He headed away from the estate until the ravine curved enough for him to cross it without being seen from the truck. Soon the binoculars scanned the truck's other side. No sign of a second man. He worked his way further back along the ravine. Half the platform's back gate lay on the ground fixed to look like the truck held nothing but hay. He could see no one up on the bed. The binoculars did reveal something ominous. Three sest of wires ran from the truck bed out into the grass in the direction of the estate.

Steve carried the Colt 1911 in the small of his back. Brothers of Sue's hammerless .32 rode above each ankle. But Steve wanted no shots fired. Then Steve noticed the big rock. The cab of the truck sat over eighteen inches deep in the ravine. A two foot diameter boulder rested at the ravine's edge by the passenger's wheel well. He could see the "farmer's" legs on the other side.

He moved back into the tall grass, then forward along the ravine. A quick peek over the grass confirmed him even with the rock. He slipped off the backpack. Then he selected two small stones and a bigger one. He moved as close to the truck as he dared. He held one .32 as his other hand threw the first stone over the man and up near the hill's crest. The man stood to look around. As he peered to the rear Steve tossed the second small stone not as far as the first one. Before the second stone hit the ground he lobbed the third just across the ravine in front of the truck.

The guard whirled toward where the second stone landed. The impact of the third stone covered Steve's five stride rush to the boulder. He put all he had into a flying leap across the hood of the truck. Focusing on the third impact the guard never heard Steve coming. If he tried to reach the Springfield, the soft ground on the far side of the truck quickly prevented it. Before the guard could recover Steve whacked the side of his head with the fist containing the small automatic. The man lay still.

With his prisoner securely gagged and tied up, Steve investigated the area under the tarp. He found three small motorcycles rigged to carry two people, an extensive medical kit for treating wounds, and boxes of ammunition. Each of the three wires led to an electric plunger detonator. They were tied to the sides of the boxes, but not connected. Each box bore a label. They read "breach wall," "crater path," and "start fire." Between two of the boxes Steve found a clipboard with a complete diagram of where the charges were and what they contained. Notes below listed signal flare colors followed by actions.

Steve dragged the prisoner back to the wind brake where he secured the man to a tree. He tossed two of the detonator boxes far into the tall grasses. As darkness fell he opened the large black box in his backpack.

He slipped on the thin black gloves. The full length black robe came next. He tucked the hem into his waistband front and back to keep it from getting caught in the vegetation. Finally he placed the unique Argus glass globe over his head and closed the hidden hinge. Thankful for the moonless night, the Moon Man strapped the remaining plunger box to his back. He headed for the estate wall winding up one strand of wire on a reel.

Maria Yardley surveyed the scene outside the mansion from the edge of the garden maze. The beautiful day's warmth began to vanish well before the sunlight. Only the hardiest of the guests and some of the chilly staff remained outside. With the showings about to begin she moved to herd all but those with the raunchiest of cigars inside.

Great City Chief of Police Peter Thatcher prowled his office scowling at the walls and everything else he saw. The convoy shepherding the replacement payroll would arrive at the Ford Plant in less than ten minutes. Most workers had elected to wait to receive immediate payment of eighty-five cents on the dollar now and the rest Monday. A huge part of the force guarded the route. His son's last minute revelation of a possible alternate target for the gang came as a shock. Nearly half of his reserve watched the approaches to the estate. If the gang struck elsewhere the department would be in serious trouble.

Herman Eisenhower watched the richly dressed people begin to gather in the horseshoe of seats in the Yardley ballroom. A moment before Maria Yardley ushered the stragglers in from outside. Smiling and polite as always yet so effective that Eisenhower pictured a sheepdog nipping at reluctant ewes in her place. Given his profession, his evening clothes matched the best there. Maria had requested that he attend, then promoted him relentlessly to those guests who truly appreciated music.

He found an out of the way seat as Mrs. Yardley took center stage. Once she held the floor he saw Maria slip out in the direction of her quarters. She really wanted no part in this "trunk show," no matter how expensive the content of that luggage.

Mrs. Yardley finished her thank yous to the guests and began the introduction of the show. "Our host tonight is here on a brief break from Broadway where he has been starring in 'Roberta' to great notices. Friends, help me welcome Mr. Bob Hope!"

The chamber music quintet played a fanfare. From the balcony a small spotlight focused on the curtains hung across an open hallway that served as the backstage area. The curtain parted. Bob Hope did not appear. Herman barely noticed the screams from the women and shouts from the men. His eyes locked on the black robed figure with a large pistol in his hand. He remembered the artist's sketch from that day's Gazette. "The Moon Man," he breathed.

The black figure with the silver mirrored head stepped to the host's microphone. The spotlight followed him closely. Slightly muffled words came out of the speakers.

"Gentlemen, please do not move. And see that your ladies do not. My men will enforce my orders with whatever force necessary. The cast of the show and the Yardley staff are tied up, or locked away. The man at the spotlight has a Browning Automatic Rifle. He can see everybody. We are going to help ourselves to what we want. If you do not try to interfere, nobody will be harmed. Men!"

From behind the curtain came four men in the familiar blue and gold uniforms. Wide brimmed cowboy hats pulled low with outlaw bandannas covered their features.

"Get started," said the glass headed leader as he placed his hand on his side arm's holster. "Just leave our friend a clear line of..."

A small shower of objects hit the floor just outside the spotlight. They bounced around with a mixed metallic clatter. Herman saw a long spring hit the leader's foot.

The spotlight widened fully. All four "cowboys" moved to shade their eyes. Flashing from above a long metal tube slammed into one man's gut. A split second later a flying wooden rifle butt removed another bandit's hat. An authoritative voice rang out. "Don't move!"

Before the five could recover a figure seemed to leap at them from the balcony near the spotlight. The flying man stopped short, in mid air, then headed for the floor and darkness. Herman heard no impact over the cries and whispers of the audience. Suddenly light blazed from the huge chandelier lighting every corner of the huge room.

Yet another man in blue and gold hung from the balcony by a thin rope around his ankles. Hands tied to his belt, his head lacked about a foot of brushing the floor as he swung back and forth.

"I said don't move!" At the head of the stairs, hand on the light switch, stood a man in an unbelted black robe. The globe on this one's head put the other's headpiece to shame. Perfect, thought Herman Eisenhower to himself. Perfect sphere. Perfect mirror.

One bandit tried to duck behind the quintet's grand piano. The heavy pistol at the top of the stairs roared. The bandit sprawled with a bullet in the thigh.

"The next one will be between the eyes!" The second figure in black held a weapon in each hand now. "The Moon Man gladly takes credit for his own crimes. But I do not tolerate the crimes of others committed in my name. You should have stuck to being General Custer. Now with your left hand, unfasten your gun belt..."

Suddenly Herman realized that a door to the balcony from the main house had eased open behind the Moon Man. A pistol held by a blue and gold clad arm appeared. Herman cried out, "Behind you! A gun!"

As he scrambled for shelter behind a huge ceramic urn Herman saw the Moon Man vault over the banister and down to the ballroom floor. The small pistol in his left hand coughed once. Splinters from the parquet floor sprayed the standing bandits freezing them.

The bandit on the balcony peered over the edge and snapped a shot at the Moon Man. The poorly aimed round exploded a section of the banister hand rail. The Moon Man fired back as he dived to one side. He hit only the ceiling. Then Herman saw a flash of movement behind the thug. The heavily weighted end of a music stand smashed into the back of the bandit's head. He cartwheeled over the balcony railing to land next to his hanging fellow. Herman smiled inwardly as he saw Maria Yardley duck back out of sight. Herman peered back around the urn. The stage curtains were falling back into place behind an empty spotlight.

The Moon Man quickly stood up. The smaller weapon disappeared. He removed the pistol from the hand of the man lying on the floor, then searched the wounded bandit. Suddenly he pointed to one of the Yardley's out of town guests. "Captain Curry," came the muffled voice. "You were a Rough Rider. Please take charge of the prisoners. There may be one or two more around. Use these," he finished, placing two pistols on a vacant chair.

With that the Moon Man dashed through the curtains. His every footfall echoed into the totally silent ballroom.

Steve sprinted down the darkened hallway. It seemed to go on forever. When he reached a door to the outside he stopped. The gang liked to protect their retreat. He opened a door off the corridor. A sitting room of some kind. Quickly he opened a window and slid outside. Blackness enveloped him. Keeping low he circled around until he could see the outside door he'd avoided. A silhouette with a cowboy hat hurried away from the door in the direction of the truck in the field.

Steve glided to the door. He found an English Mills bomb attached to the knob. He cut the string to the detonator and brought the device with him. Fifty yards down the trail of the bandits he pulled the pin and heaved the grenade back toward the mansion.

The flash of the explosion lit the area ahead of him like a flash bulb. Four figures hurried towards the estate wall. Steve angled away from the gang. He put on as much speed as he dared in the darkness to a huge oak tree surrounded by stone benches and tables he discovered on his way in.

He reached under one bench as he heard popping sound. A moment later a red flare came to life in the sky. The demolitions card said "red flare = breach wall now." The gang would be on the ground or behind trees for safety. Steve hurriedly attached the wires to the plunger box retrieved from under the bench. Moving behind the huge oak he rammed home the plunger.

Thunder and lightning split the night. As soon as the shock wave passed him The Moon Man dashed for the heavy stone wall.

The gang members emerged from cover to hurry forward to the estate wall. Then one tripped and fell cursing into a shallow, but hot crater. From their right a chilling voice came out of the darkness, "The wall still stands. Surrender, or die!"

The Moon Man watched the shadowy forms freeze momentarily. Then pistol rounds began whizzing by him. Others impacted the two foot diameter elm tree he used for cover. He fired at the muzzle flashes from first the left side of the tree, then the right.

His first volley brought a scream of pain. If these were former enlisted soldiers the Moon Man reasoned their fighting marksmanship experience would be with rifles, not hand guns. He fired another volley from each hand.

He fell to the ground before looking out again. Shots passed over his head. The two remaining forms backed towards the wall firing as they went. Their muzzle flashes were suddenly reflected from something at the top of the wall. The flashes from the glass helm of the false Moon Man revealed that he straddled the top of the stones.

The real Moon Man triggered both automatics at the impostor from the prone position. The smaller .32 caliber's slide locked back empty just as the false Moon Man dived to the far side of the wall and safety.

Steve rose from the grass. He holstered the empty weapon and drew his third pistol in a quick fluid motion. He fired once at the two bandits near the wall, then slid a fresh clip into the Model 1911.

He could not let the phony Moon Man get away. Throwing caution, or what was left of it, to the winds, he charged. He kept firing as he swept down on the two. They fired back. More than once he felt the tug of bullets on his wide cloak. One round screamed past the globe of Argus glass so closely that it hummed like a tuning fork.

His charge ended as he looked down at two badly wounded men. The third was clearly dead. Hurriedly he collected their weapons. Then tossed them over the wall. That brought a volley of shots on the far side of the wall.

The Moon Man holstered his weapons. He dashed ten steps along the wall then leaped up the rough finished stone work. The fingers of one hand found purchase. Swaying wildly he pulled out the small folding grappling hook that got him over the wall the first time. A desperate throw nearly cost him his grip, then the hook bit into something. On pure adrenalin the Moon Man swarmed to the top.

Colt automatic in hand he lay prone on the wall's top. Back at the breach point of the wall he suddenly realized that he could see the constellation Orion in a patch of brush. He fired just as the stars moved.

The near miss finished the stand of the false Moon Man. He fled back towards the truck in a broken field run worthy of Red Grange.

The true Moon Man lay on the wall. He aimed ahead of the fleeing man. He aimed at a piece of white paper topped by a rock at the limit of accurate pistol range. With a small prayer he emptied the magazine.

The sixth round hit the gang's cratering charge. Only the grapnel line wrapped around his arm kept the Moon Man atop the wall. Only the fine craftsmanship of the thick Argus glass kept the globe intact.

Shaking his head to clear it, Steve climbed down to the far side. He found the body of Major Albright sprawled back at the foot of the wall. Glass shards surrounded the man's head.

Steve felt exhausted, but he could not rest. Both he and the Moon Man needed to make phone calls. Plus, he had a long drive ahead. As he collected his backpack Steve tried to remember if he had left that Baby Ruth bar in the La Salle.

Steve woke as the rising crescent moon shone in his eyes. He struck a match to check the dashboard clock. Only two hours till dawn. He mashed the La Salle's starter. As the engine roared to life, he decided he would enjoy sitting down to breakfast with the Angel.

THE END

GETTING A HANDLE
ON THE MOON MAN

Oh joy! I said when I first started this story; a real writing assignment. Oh my? I had never before written a story to a specific length. And the wife and I are going on our first vacation without the kids in thirty years. How will I get anything done staying with her sister in Orlando? Her husband spends a lot of time on their system. I'd have to use the computer while he's asleep. I've got my son's 1998 laptop that he bought for deployment to Bosnia, but the hard drive is dead.

Let's see... The Moon Man! The Moon Man? I've got a couple of stories sitting in my collection. Been there for more than twenty years. Never read 'em. Here they are. Fillers in Weinberg's Pulp Classics behind The Whisperer and somebody else. I read them and immediately get the story titles and the plots backwards. Then I'm loaned a couple more stories. Helps.

Bit of a question here. How can the Moon Man fight crime when he actually commits them? Steve Thatcher is paid to chase bad guys. Hummmmmm... This puts me in mind of of a story in one of the later issues of the Black Hood's comic. Turned out to be a blindly recycled Hangman story.

Uniformed Patrolman Kip Burland and girl friend go into a department store. Guess what? They find an armed robbery in progress. Does Kip yank out his service revolver? No. Does he shout "Halt! Police!?" Not hardly. Kip ducks behind a display counter to dump his uniform and perfectly legal pistol. Then he goes hand to hand with crooks using firearms. Hold the phone?!?!?!

Why would the Moon Man risk capture going against criminals that Steve should be trying to take down. Only one reason: The Moon Man's reputation is at stake. Ergo, I create a phony Moon Man.

Vacation's coming up soon. I find time to bang out two single spaced pages. I print and pack them. Now for the dead Windblow$ 98 laptop. Our son gamed his way through eight months with it in out in the middle of nowhere Bosnia. It has seen better days. Oh, and the hard drive's dead.

Now here's something I've been wanting to try: Puppy Linux. Download and burn the ISO CD image. Put CD in laptop with USB drive attached to save files and settings. Power up. I'll be darned, it works. Ninety-some total megs of ram and forty-four are available to run programs. The connection gizmo figures out Road Runner in about thirty seconds. Abi-Word is more than enough for my needs. As a bonus the battery is still good for an hour or so.

On the plane from Kansas City to Orlando I outline the whole story while playing pseudo-granddad to a sweet seven year old traveling alone.

For the last fifteen years I've had flextime at work. That means I can and do start as early as 6:00AM. In Orlando this turns out to be a great benefit. I get up one to two hours ahead of everyone. I take the laptop out on the patio and manage five hundred words most mornings. I create Patrolman Reynolds with the film "Electra-Glide In Blue" in mind. That starred Robert Blake. By the time I finish the story all I can see and hear for Reynolds is Joe Pesci.

As part of our anniversary celebration the wife and I go to the one theme park we've never been to before: MGM-Disney. And two pulp things happened to me. First I'm selected to be in the cast of the Indiana Jones Stunt Spectacular. Great fun. How pulp can you get?! Later, on one of the streets I discover a La Salle roadster of proper vintage on display. I take a couple of digital pictures. Guess what Steve Thatcher drives in my story.

Back home I keep pounding away, but in a less structured way. After a week or two it feels a bit aimless. Maybe instead of happening in one day, the case should take up two. Or... Maybe...

Writer slaps forehead. Remembers existence of outline. Checks outline. Ohhhhh, right... Rearranges elements. Bumps "retired" safe cracker from mid-morning to afternoon. Creates a couple of throwaway characters one of whom turns out to be the mastermind.

References and ideas spring into my head. Are they authentic to the period. (M*A*S*H, one of my all time favorite TV shows, once showed Radar asleep in his bunk covered with 1960's Marvel Comics.) These days the net makes things easy. Yes, Red Grange played football in the 1920's. Google even rescued me once, "Did you mean Andy Frain?" Gee, for forty years I thought the usher service was named Andy Frame.

I learn things on these fact finding missions. I didn't know that Tiffany's redesigned the pyramid seal on the dollar bill, or that the U.S. government adopted their definition of sterling silver as the official national standard.

As I wind up the story I throw in a few cameo appearances by real people.

Finally, the story has ended. The spell checker quits complaining. Done!

ERWIN K. ROBERTS - believes that heroes of all kinds, real and fictional, have always been important, remain important, and will always be important.

I am one of the last middle class Americans who remembers a home without a television. My interests in science fiction, fantasy, and masked men, began by listening to the radio. I remember the radio version of Space Patrol, and Big John & Sparky on Saturday mornings. Three nights a week I listened to the Lone Ranger. The other two to Sergeant Preston of the Yukon. I thought the TV's Sky King was a wimp. After all, the radio version owned both the Songbird, plus a jet. And both planes were armed!

I have loved comics ever since my Grandmother read to me "Only A Poor Old Man" from my sister's Uncle Scrooge #1. (That comic is long gone, but I do have her copy of The Cisco Kid #1.)

The first movie I remember seeing is Disney's live-action version of Robin Hood. (There's a pattern here, isn't there?)

I hold degrees in Graphic Arts & Communications.

From 1982 through 1998 I appeared on, wrote for, produced, and occasionally directed access/community cable television. In the early 1990's I hosted the WBE-TV Network's "Action Theater" under the alias "Major A.D. Venture." I have been a film critic for over twenty-five years in the Kansas City metro area.

A retired Army National Guard NCO, I earn part of my living creating computer graphics and training aids for a government agency.

I can be reached at erwin.k.roberts@gmail.com.

FIRE AND GLASS
By Ken Janssens

*I*t's the simple things that make life worth living. Tonight, for Detective Sergeant Stephen Thatcher, it was having a beer at Finley's Pub with his father. Stephen hoisted his Beverwyck Irish Cream to his lips and watched Chief of Police Peter Thatcher relax back against the bar. It had been a hard two months. Jewelry heists were on the rise, baffling the entire Great City police force. Undoubtedly, the Moon Man was behind them, which was the conclusion whenever a criminal could not be identified or apprehended. The thefts stopped about two weeks ago, allowing Peter and Stephen to take a night off to enjoy the fine view of red-haired lasses bounding around in their afternoon dresses a few hours too late.

Stephen took note of his father's white hair as he stole a puff from his pipe. Now that he really examined it, Peter's coif seemed to have receded more of late. Stephen felt a sense of guilt over the stress the chief of police was going through. The Moon Man was making Peter's life hell.

It was all a part of the plan, however. Not the fact that his father's health was being affected, but the perception that Moon Man was the worst menace that Great City had ever known. Stephen had planned it that way. It was a ploy to get closer to the criminal element of the city and put them out of commission... while availing them of their ill-gotten gains so he could redistribute them among the needy and wronged. Rob from the jaded rich, give to the good poor. The archer of Sherwood Forest would be proud.

The Moon Man was taking its toll on Stephen as well. The detective sergeant was athletic and a top-notch shot. His grueling double life as police officer and the Moon Man was making him lose weight and the recent tired vision had thrown his aim off by inches. That may not sound like much but it was the difference between shooting a pistol out of a villain's hand and firing a bullet through a damsel's heart.

71

That's why tonight was such a welcome break. The Bulgarian jewel thieves were dealt with. The gems, rings, and necklaces were anonymously returned back to their owners. The extra money that couldn't be brought back to where it was taken, found its way to a group of homeless men.

Stephen was sure in need of some unwinding. A cool ale, the company of his father, the only thing that could make this better was some fun exercise to stretch out the muscles.

"Don't make thisss harder on youse." A loud, slurring baritone resonated through the noisy bar, causing all conversation to stop. Stephen and Peter eyed two tall, skinny men with party masks over their faces threaten Stanley, the bartender. The man with the bright red hair wearing a denim jacket held an old Baby Hammerless 22RF up to the obese drink-slinger's chin. The more frenetic robber, who had a long wrench as his weapon, bounced up and down on his heels, his pupils darting everywhere around the room. Stephen was glad that the latter one wasn't holding the pistol. With the amount of drugs running through his veins, by now the antique would have already fired due to excessive twitching.

"He'll hurt you, buddy," said the vibrating accomplice, not making eye contact with anyone in particular.

The detective sergeant turned his head around to gauge his father's willingness to take on the unscrupulous scoundrels. He got his answer right away in the form of a wide smile. Stephen began to stumble over towards the men who watched the shorter Stanley rummage through his cash register till. Twitchy was the first one to notice him.

"What's you doing, maggot?" he asked nervously, rocking the wrench on his finger tips.

"Are you our waiter?" Stephen said sloppily, attracting the attention of the ruffian with the Hammerless as well. " 'Cause I haven't seen a gin come my way in five whole minutes."

"Back up, ya lusssh." Now the pistol was pointed at Stephen. As the Moon Man, this wouldn't bother him much. Even as a regular police officer, he would have his firearm trained back on the lisper, forcing him to drop his. Currently, the only things Stephen had on his side were the belief that this guy didn't want to shoot anyone and the hope that he could verbally stall for ten more seconds.

"Hey, whoa, I'm going to leave a tip this time," Stephen replied, pretending to teeter back and forth but actually positioning himself so his weight transferred to his toes. "I swear. I've got this bet going on the Tigers and I just know it's a sure thing this–"

An elbow flew into the face of the red-headed bandit as a slightly wrinkled hand snatched the Hammerless before it could go off. Chief of Police Thatcher had maneuvered himself around the bar and behind the tall, masked man. The uncanny stealth of his old man's actions impressed Stephen greatly. He didn't let his pride slow him down in the least. Springing forward, Stephen tackled the heroin-infused thief, making him juggle his weapon and lose it as it soared into the shocked crowd. Both men flew across the room in the tussle and slammed into a round table. A leg broke as it toppled, and Stephen flipped over Twitchy, landing on his back. Like a leopard, the thief was on top of Stephen with fists wailing on the detective sergeant's face. His arms might have been pinned under his assailant's knees but Stephen's legs were loose and immediately his ankles were wrapped around the tall man's neck. He straightened out, causing the robber's back to arch. With a swivel of his hips, the masked hoodlum was thrown to the side and into the wall. A hanging, hefty, wood crest broke away from the single nail that secured it between two small windows, finishing the job as it landed on Twitchy's head.

Peter didn't have a chance to enjoy his son's agile move. After a struggle with the gun that resulted in it sliding under the bar itself, the chief of police was locked in an exchange of fisticuffs. They traded blows like prize pugilists competing for the heavy weight belt. If Peter's sixty plus years were a disadvantage, it wasn't apparent. A good right hook under the redhead's eye helped skew the fight in the top cop's favor as it instantly puffed up to blur his vision. Peter took this opportunity to take out the former gunman's left knee with a well placed kick. The lanky man collapsed down to half his height. The end of the melee was punctuated by the chief of police pushing the bandit's face into the hardwood.

"Who's got some rope?" Peter called.

"I can do you one better, Chief" sounded a familiar voice. The chief of police looked up to see Lieutenant Gilbert McEwen passing him a pair of handcuffs. Through the puff of cigar smoke hovering around his head, McEwen looked around to see the damage caused. He was sad that he had missed the fight. McEwen stuck out his hand once Peter had cuffed the bumbling bandit, and his boss used it to hoist himself up.

"Stopping in for a drink, Lieutenant?" questioned the chief as he straightened his rumpled shirt.

"I wish that was the case, but it's not." The dire tone in McEwen's voice let on that his reason for being at the bar was purely business. The leather-faced lieutenant was already rattling off details about a downtown fire as

Stephen carted his sparring partner over.

"The crowd that assembled said that the fire consumed the shop in minutes," the restless, fifty-year-old-Irish cop related. His cigar was almost all the way down to the nub but he kept puffing.

"The speed makes you think it was arson?" Stephen asked his superior.

"The ten empty cans of turpentine in the back alley makes me think it was arson, Thatcher."

"Was anyone killed?"

"No, the place was closed and the owner wasn't there at the time."

"What kind of business was it?"

"A cigar shop, Chief," McEwen said stoically.

"Ironic," quipped Stephen.

"Well, Gil, I assume that you need something from me since you came all the way down here."

"Believe it or not, I came here for Stephen."

Stephen looked at the lieutenant with confusion. McEwen didn't usually go out of his way to seek out Stephen's advice when the junior detective had the day off. Of late, they hadn't even been on the friendliest of terms. The dual life of the Moon Man had bled over into the Bulgarian case and Stephen had to 'secretly' put a few obstacles in the lieutenant's way. Hopefully, McEwen wasn't catching on to the Moon Man's alter ego after all these years.

"The shop owner says he knows you," the detective went on. "'Rudy Petersen' ring a bell?"

"Yeah, and I'd like to ring his."

The pre-dawn moon reflected off Stephen's Argus helmet as he skulked down the back alley. He was now the Moon Man; draped in a black cloak, black gloves, and peering through the one-way glass surrounding his head. The Moon Man made sure that all the police had gone home before he maneuvered his way into the crime scene of rubble and smoke.

There was charred wood everywhere. Ashes still danced in the air, their flight quickened by the wind created by the Moon Man's movements. A building housing smoking papers, leaves, and wooden humidors. It never stood a chance.

While he scanned around to find the point where the fire started, Stephen thought of the last time he saw Rudy Petersen. It was seven years ago. Rudy and Stephen were pals in college and better friends after. That's until they met Amy Byrne. Stephen mused how quickly love could turn friends into rivals.

The Moon Man followed the beam of his flashlight, circling back to the point he had entered to end his search. Blackened glass shards rested upon the floor where the charring was the heaviest. The V-shaped pattern was basically an arrow pointing right to this spot. The Moon Man was hit by the scent of the turpentine. Whoever started the fire probably broke the glass of the window, dumped in the fuel, then lit the match. The Moon Man's flashlight glimmered off a corner of melted metal under one of the darkened shards. Bouncing the metal around his fingers to make sure it wasn't too hot, the Moon Man examined it closer. The side that had been facing up was indistinguishable but the bottom clearly told Stephen what he was holding. It was a Zippo lighter. There was an engraving on the back that was slightly warped but still readable. The initials were R.I.P.

The Moon Man placed the Zippo back where he found it, knowing that when McEwen and a few of his men returned in the morning after the ash had settled, they would find it. As the Moon Man gave the area a final look over, he mused about the morbidity of the initials. His first thought, of course, was that a message might have been sent. Rest In Peace. But quickly, another notion popped into his domed head. They were a person's initials. A person he was going to see at headquarters in a few hours; Mr. Rudolf Ignatius Petersen.

First thing the next morning, Stephen, McEwen, and the prematurely balding Rudy Petersen sat in the lieutenant's office. Rudy's demeanor was cordial and inviting, obviously trying to elicit favorable treatment from his former friend. He hoped that their falling out wouldn't still be an issue. That hope didn't last.

"Like a cigar, Rudy?" Stephen asked, aware that the man across from him would take it as antagonistic. Stephen believed it might even help the questioning.

"That some kind of joke, Stephen?" Rudy snarled. "I just lost my entire smoke shop, my livelihood."

"Sorry, I wasn't thinking," Stephen responded. "I was only trying to calm you down. Here."

Rudy hesitantly took the extended stogie while the lieutenant watched him.

"Aren't going to share with the rest of the class?" McEwen growled, his well known love of cigars being slighted at this moment.

"I only had the one."

"Got a light?" Rudy asked.

"I thought you'd carry around a fancy Zippo or something."

"I left mine at a bar a few nights ago. When I remembered it and went back, someone had already swiped it. Haven't picked out a new one yet."

"Here," offered McEwen with a pack of matches. Rudy started puffing away, and it did indeed seem to cut away his edginess. "What bar was that?" Stephen asked.

"The Hessian on Smith," Rudy stated, his look relating his confusion over the relevance. McEwen was starting to get annoyed so he took over the interview. Stephen was okay with this, now that he had a lead to follow up.

"Do you have any enemies, Mr. Petersen?"

"Not that I know of."

"How about any debts?"

"Wait, what are you implying?"

"You burn down your own shop, Mr. Petersen?" the lieutenant inquired without any change in his tone.

"No, absolutely not!" Rudy turned to the man he once called 'brother' and tried to find a lifeline. "Stephen, we've had our differences in the past but you know me. This isn't something I'd do."

"I don't know. There were a lot of things about you that I was wrong about." Stephen regretted saying that. Actually, looking at Rudy now, he was pretty sure that he was telling the truth. R.I.P.'s life wasn't going to get any easier, though. McEwen's men would be stumbling across that Zippo at any moment.

"So we're not going to find any evidence at your shop that suggests otherwise, huh?" It was like McEwen was reading Stephen's thoughts. Stephen disliked Rudy, but the Moon Man was going to have to prove his innocence with a little help from his true friends.

Ned Dargan strolled into the Hessian as the sun was starting to fall behind the skyline. This man knew what it was like to get into a fight. With a nose broken several times and cauliflower ears that had been boxed too often to count, Ned would make anyone gulp in worry just by looking at him. That was the reason the Moon Man had sent him to the Hessian.

Ned, affectionately known as "Angel", was many things to the Moon Man. Friend, driver, loyal aide, and tonight, intimidator. Angel ambled over to the bartender and ordered a bar whiskey. He took one sip then addressed the bartender with a booming voice that he hoped reached every corner of the room.

"Fella by the name of Rudy Petersen came in here a few nights back," Angel roared. "Who was he drinking with?"

"Don't know anybody by that name," the bartender returned without fear. A man had to have a stiff backbone if he was going to run a joint like this one.

"Then how about a face," Angel continued. "Roundish but with a pointy chin, balding hair."

"So no different than half the people that are in here right now."

"This guy also had his cigar shop burnt down last night."

"That's the guy who left his lighter the other night. Yeah, he was arse-faced drunk as can be. First time I'd seen him."

"Do you remember who he was with?" Angel raised his voice louder.

"Wouldn't have much of a business if I remembered things like that," the bartender answered. With that, the front door to the bar opened. Angel was able to catch out of the corner of his eye a man in a trench coat leaving in a bit of hurry. Pounding back the rest of his whiskey, he celebrated a job well done.

Sue McEwen wasn't like many women of the day. For starters, she carried a pearl handled automatic in her purse. She was brilliant, independent, and a young beauty in her twenties. Sue also happened to be the only other person on the planet, besides Angel, who knew Stephen's alter ego.

As a man in a trench coat briskly exited the Hessian, Sue started to trail after him, aware that her part had started. The daughter of Lieutenant Gil McEwen attempted to keep the clicking of her heels on the pavement to a minimum, not wanting to alert the man with the upturned collar. But what did it matter? Sue was just a sweet lady going for a walk.

Sue took to memory as many attributes of her prey as she could. The man had a full coif of black hair peeking out the top, his height was an average five-nine, five-ten maybe. He was slender, but by no means scrawny, and never let up his speed, to the point that she was starting to lag too far behind. There were enough people still on the sidewalks, as well as a fair amount of cars on the street, that Sue felt she could clip along at a faster rate. She kept up with him for another four blocks, then the fleeing man stopped.

Sue halted in her tracks. The man in the trench coat turned his head around. Dusk was blanketing Great City and all the lieutenant's daughter could discern were the man's eyes locking on hers. The mutual glare lasted a second, seemingly impossible to break. And then he was off.

Sprinting like a man whose shoes were on fire, the runner traveled two blocks in no time, his trench coat billowing up behind him. He whipped around a corner and darted down a blackened back alley. The pain to his stomach came out of nowhere as all the air in his lungs left him. The man toppled to the ground several yards from the spot where he was punched in the gut.

The Moon Man was quickly on him to put him down permanently. His plan was to knock him unconscious then bring him somewhere secure and private. Regrettably, the Moon Man didn't see the thick splinter of wood in the trench coat man's hand.

The howl of Stephen's scream echoed inside his helmet. The wood was firmly lodged into his thigh, and with only one leg to stand on, the Moon Man slumped against the wall. He reached for his gun to keep his quarry from dashing off but it was too late.

"Oh no!" Sue cried as she glimpsed the spike protruding out of the man she loved. "Stephen!"

"Get Ned... unnnhhhh... to bring the car around." As he uttered those last words, the Moon Man passed out from agony.

A gash of light poured into the spreading eyelids of Stephen Thatcher. The Argus helmet was removed as were his pants. In fact, every stitch of clothing that identified Stephen as the Moon Man had been removed and now he rested at Great City General Hospital. After he adjusted to the brightness of the room, he took in the collection of mostly familiar faces that surrounded his bed. Along with Sue, Chief Thatcher and Lieutenant McEwen stirred as Stephen did the same. A nurse was also there, checking his vitals as he noticed the large bandage encompassing his thigh.

Several hours passed as smiles were exchanged by everyone. Even the lieutenant was definitively happy, an emotion he barely expressed around Stephen over the last few weeks. Soon, Sue was asleep on a chair across the room and Stephen's father went to get food. That left Stephen alone with the master interrogator.

"Can't remember anything about the guy?" Gil questioned, having been fed a story involving a mugger attack during a walk home from a romantic dinner with his daughter.

"It must be the shock," Stephen lied, feeling bad as he did it. Though, lies to his friends and family were nothing new to him. A sense of guilt washed over 'the Moon Man'. It was never easy. It was only necessary.

"I got a confession to make, Stephen."

"Okay," the patient hesitated.

"I've been a little angry with you for the past several weeks. You went against me on the warrant I tried to get out of Judge Severs for the Bulgarian case. It hurt me." McEwen paused. Admitting he acted foolish was not easy for a hard man like him. "But I have to admit that you were right. You're a good man, Stephen. You treat my daughter right and you'll never let her get harmed. You're a man of integrity, Stephen. And the most honest person, I know... I'm sorry."

Stephen's sense of guilt changed from a wash to a flood.

Three days later, Stephen hobbled into his precinct. The doctors said it would take a month or so to get off his crutches, longer to have full mobility back in his leg. Stephen was determined to shorten that timeline immensely. He had to.

Rudy peered down at his shoes as Stephen watched him through the bars. McEwen's men had found the Zippo. They also had a witness that placed Rudy at the cigar shop minutes before it was consumed with flames. Rudy's arraignment was tomorrow but today he had nowhere to go, nothing to do but answer Stephen's questions.

The jail guard brought a chair over for Stephen to sit down on. Rudy's head jerked up when he realized he had company.

"Not your week," Stephen said, referencing a bygone private joke between the two former classmates.

"Not my week," Rudy smirked. The old connection sparked for a brief second. "What happened to your leg?"

"Cut myself shaving."

"..I think you're innocent..."

"You really were bad at the grooming process," Rudy quipped.

"Tell me about it," Stephen volleyed back.

"You come to grill me on my nefarious deeds?"

"I hate to say this but I think you're innocent."

Rudy was shocked. He stood up and approached the cold, vertical steel that separated them.

"You do. Does that mean I'm free to go?"

"No," Stephen said with genuine remorse. He had Sue now and was happy. It was time to put past grudges where they belonged; in the past. "I'm sorry but even though I think you're innocent, no one else does. For that, I'm going to need enough evidence to prove it."

"What can I do?"

"Who did you drink with the last time you were at the Hessian?"

"I was there by myself."

"And you didn't have a drink with anyone?"

"No."

Stephen's eyes penetrated into Rudy's skull. The man who won Amy's heart all those years ago had never been a good liar.

"I was there waiting for a... woman," said Rudy, readjusting his story.

"Amy?"

"Nah, we split years ago. Truthfully, I haven't had much luck with the ladies since." Rudy rubbed his balding scalp.

Stephen felt even sorrier for the guy. "You're saying that this was a prostitute?"

"I can plead the fifth here, right?" The two men shared another smirk.

"When did she show up?"

"She never did. I waited for hours. When I finally left, I was completely soused." Rudy's face fell, knowing that Stephen was looking for more than that. Then a flicker of memory shot through his brain and rejuvenated his features. "There was a guy who came and sat with me at the bar for ten or fifteen minutes. Bought me a drink."

"What can you tell me about him?"

"Geez, not a lot. Black hair."

"Did he wear a trench coat?"

"Yeah," Rudy strained. "Yeah, I'm pretty sure he did. Do you know who it was?"

"No," Stephen said as he picked himself off the chair, using his crutches as leverage. "But I'm going to find out. You got someone to post bail for you tomorrow?"

"Yeah, my dad and brother."

"Great," the detective retorted solemnly. "Make sure you stay with one of them. Don't go back to your home. It might not be safe."

The implication of those words sent new worries skirting through Rudy's mind. There might be a man out there that wanted to murder him.

Stephen awkwardly made his way to the detective department of the precinct. McEwen was sitting at his desk, miserably digging through piles of paperwork.

"What's the deal with the witness for the Petersen case?" Stephen asked McEwen. The premier sleuth smiled between puffs of his cigar to see his friend up and around so quickly.

"Can't keep a bad man down, huh?" The lieutenant flipped through a few files until he reached what he was looking for. "Arthur Gold. Sixty-year old. Lives on Holland."

Stephen accepted the folder from McEwen and browsed through it.

"Mind if I have a word with this guy?"

"You think you can do better than Mackenzie?"

"What else am I good for right now?"

"Well, playing canasta for one," McEwen suggested. "Shouldn't you be taking it easy? Doctor's orders or something."

"The last three days in the hospital drove me crazy enough."

"Knock yourself out."

Stephen stepped out of the Cadillac Sixteen onto Holland Boulevard. Once he had approached the Mackenzies' front door, Angel, his chauffeur, drove out of sight. Stephen knocked repeatedly on the door. A short, blond man in his early sixties came to the door, unimpressed with the disturbance.

"And you are...?" Mr. Gold asked impatiently. The sound of Orson Welles as The Shadow echoed over the radio. Stephen was interrupting the man's stories.

"Detective Stephen Thatcher."

"About the fire? I already talked to the police about that."

"This is just a follow up," Stephen insisted. "If you wouldn't mind..."

Arthur Gold knew that the enjoyment of his radio show was over, flicking off the radio as both men sat down in the living room. Mr. Gold pulled out a cigarette and offered one to Stephen, who politely declined.

"It says in the report that you saw Mr. Petersen leaving his shop only minutes before the blaze. Where was he leaving?"

"The shop," Mr. Gold said with confusion.

"No, did he just walk out the front door?"

"He came out the back door," the sexagenarian answered coolly.

"And he took both of his cans of gasoline with him?"

"I wasn't close enough and it was too dark to see if they were gasoline, but yeah."

Stephen stared at Mr. Gold. It was no longer time to play the nice cop. "That's interesting because he left ten cans of turpentine in the back lane. Why would he take two cans away and not the rest?"

"Maybe he was going to come back for the rest but ran out of time." Mr. Gold's expression didn't change at all but Stephen could determine a slight change in his voice.

"You said you couldn't make out what kind of cans he was carrying. How could you be sure it was Mr. Petersen?"

"I can recognize the man I buy smokes from." Mr. Gold puffed heavily on his cigarette, blowing rings out to illustrate his mock ease.

"That's odd. Because I did a little research before I came here and you have a standing account with Top Line Tobacconists." That was it. Mr. Gold knew that Stephen him skillfully trapped him in a lie. The older man's eyes skirted around the room. Stephen didn't know if he was looking for a gun or an exit; neither would help. Stephen pulled out his thirty-eight revolver.

"Who paid you to fake your testimony?" He demanded. It was obvious that this old geezer wasn't the raven-haired runner that bested him the other day.

"I don't know his name," Gold quivered.

"You'll have to do better."

"I can tell you who he worked for – the guy who paid me off – but..."

"...you need reassurances," Stephen finished. "Tell me who bought your testimony and it will be like I was never here. Scout's honor."

"You're a scout who is holding a gun on me," Mr. Gold retorted.

"Nevertheless."

"This can never come back to me otherwise I'm dead. You understand?" Stephen nodded agreement. "Jules Popper."

"Mobster Julie, "Pop Bang," Popper?"

"That's the guy. Now will you please get out of here?"

"I bet Popper's thug didn't give you a reason why he wanted you to lie."

"You would win that bet," Mr. Gold said as he turned the last couple minutes of The Shadow back on.

Angel, Sue, and Stephen gathered around the kitchen table in Angel's apartment. Sue was tending to Stephen's bandages as they all discussed their next step.

"Julie Popper," Angel ruminated. "That's one big fish."

"With bigger pockets," Stephen mused.

"If you were more like Robin Hood right now and less like Hopalong Cassidy, I might be able to get behind this. However, I don't see the Moon Man hobbling into the Jewish mob's secret headquarters and having his way with one of the most vicious criminals in Great City."

"And I'm not going to let him," Sue interjected as she cinched Stephen's bandages tight.

"Popper isn't like other gangsters anyway," Stephen grimaced, wiggling his leg free of Sue's hands. "To find him and figure out the best way to 'chat' with him is going to take weeks of investigating, staking out, and the like. By that time, I should be as good as new."

"I don't know about that," challenged Angel.

"I do," deadpanned Stephen.

The next few weeks were some of the most taxing of Stephen's life. During the days, he worked on his leg with a physical therapist, pushing himself to the limit. Nights were spent trailing members of the Jewish mafia, following up leads attained by Angel while spending time in some of the less reputable establishments in the city, and trudging through all the files the police department had on Popper and his lieutenants. Stephen's vacation from the force was filled with sweat and pain. His mental faculties were wearing down. His sleep was often interrupted. His leg burned every waking moment. But seventeen days later, Sgt. Stephen Thatcher was in a kosher deli, eating pastrami on rye, sitting four tables away from Isaac Bloom, Pop Bang's right-hand man.

Stephen rubbed his thigh as it was cramping a tad. He had been sitting in there for almost an hour, waiting for Bloom to show up. Stephen no longer needed the crutches. Though, he used a walking stick now, he didn't require it for small treks. Heck, he could even jog a couple of blocks, unaided, but the pain afterwards required a stiff drink to dull the ache.

Once he finished his Thursday ritual of two potato knishes and a Coca-

Cola, Bloom got up from his seat, dropped a bill on the table, and yelled into the kitchen his compliments to the chef.

The large, square-jawed mobster lurched out the door with Stephen right behind him.

Bloom kept up a swift pace. This was his natural gait, not an indication that he was aware of being tailed. After seven blocks, he turned down Blue Nun Avenue for a block then entered the lobby of a ritzy apartment building. Stephen, hurting from the quick stroll, let Bloom open the front door and disappear before he approached. Bloom had used a key so the odds were this was his residence.

Stephen scanned the names on the bronze foyer call box to find 'Bloom' but it wasn't there. There was, however, a 'Daniel Rose' in the penthouse.

The Moon Man peered into Bloom's apartment from the marble-railed balcony. The strain caused from utilizing only his arm strength to climb the six stories with a grappling hook rope prompted him to doubt the intelligence of the endeavor. Though every limb was sore, he still had his forty-five automatic to back him up. The window slid open quietly as the Moon Man squeezed in, muzzle first. The living room was unoccupied. From the look of the décor, Bloom didn't want for much.

The Moon Man headed towards the bedroom. The light was on but nobody was in the main area. A private bathroom protruded off to the side and rumblings were emanating from it. The Moon Man crept across the room and stopped to listen to the sprinkling shower. He entered and rested against the sink counter while Bloom cleaned the day off. The agony of lifting himself up all those flights was worth the surprise on Bloom's face when he finally noticed the Moon Man.

"What the hell??!" Bloom cried out as he wrapped a towel around his waist.

"That's the last move you make without being rewarded with an extra eye socket."

"I would say 'don't you know who I am?' but I gather that you do." Bloom didn't seem bothered with being defenseless against a masked, and armed, villain. He knew of the notorious Moon Man; reputation traveled fast in Great City.

"Let's make this quick then. What do you want?"

"Information," the Moon Man answered. "Tell me about your

involvement in a fire that occurred a few weeks back. Cigar shop."

"What's it to you?"

"What's the number one mob rule?"

"The mope with the gun gets to ask the questions," answered Bloom, familiar with the motto. The mobster wrenched his neck to one side so he could crack it then proceeded. "Not much really."

"How much?" The Moon Man stood straight to emphasize his patience was being tried.

"Friend wanted a witness. I provided one."

"A fake witness. Why?"

"You better be fast," Bloom said at the same time he whipped the towel off his body and onto the Moon Man's helmet. The Moon Man let off a shot but it didn't hit its mark. By the time he could see again, it was too late. Two sharp punches to the Moon Man's ribcage toppled him over. His index finger compressed the trigger a second time with better results. Blood splattered out the back of Bloom's shoulder as he raced out of the bathroom. The Moon Man was right behind him. A third shot went off but missed and Bloom sprinted into the living room. Aching everywhere, the Moon Man gave chase. He was greeted by bullets as the naked mobster had grabbed a revolver to defend himself.

Bloom used his plush couch for cover. The Moon Man used the wall as he shot through the doorway. Whenever one thought he had a good crack at hitting the other, he let loose a slug. The Moon Man ran out first but played that he still had ammo. He coerced the final two bullets out of Bloom's revolver then stepped into the living room. The two men confronted at each other. They were going to lock horns; the when depended on who charged first.

The Moon Man stormed towards the middle of the room, ignoring the pain that coursed through him. Bloom quickly parroted the move. The collision would be fantastic but the pure heft of the mobster indicated that he would create a more forceful impact. The vigilante in the billowing cloak knew that, so when they were about to clash, he used Detective Thatcher's thirty-eight pistol, shooting Bloom in the kneecap. That stopped the big man in his tracks but the Moon Man kept on coming. He tackled Bloom pushing him back into the window.

The smashing of glass and the splintering of wood echoed through the alley below as both men dropped onto the thick oak of the sixth-story balcony. Bloom was dazed and cut up badly. The Moon Man shoved the thirty-eight into Bloom's nostril as the criminal breathed heavily. Blood oozed out of his two bullet holes.

"Okay," the Moon Man panted, the wind knocked out of him. "One more time with feeling. Why was the Cigar Shop burnt down?"

"I... I can't tell you the why," Jules Popper's number two spit out, accompanied by gobs of blood. "I can tell you who."

Whether Bloom would have told the Moon Man the answer or not, gravity had other plans in mind. The oak of the balcony was too sturdy to break, even from the plummeting weight of the two men lying on top of it. The brackets, screws, nails, and the pine studs, however, were not. The cracking of the balcony away from the wall was deafening.

Seconds felt like hours; both men's eyes would have been locked onto one another if Bloom could see Stephen's through the Argus glass. With everything he had left in him, the Moon Man sprung backwards and grasped onto the remnants of the window pane. Bloom started to ride the balcony down when a last ditch flailing ended with the mobster's baseball-mitt-of-a-hand gripping the Moon Man's foot.

Lightning snaked through Stephen's thigh as it tried to hold the weight of 'Daniel Rose'. It felt like the shard of wood had been plunged back into his leg. Bloom looked up at him for mercy... or because there was nothing else to do. Either the Moon Man's leg would rip away from his body or his shoe would slip loose. It was the latter. And no matter how strong Pop Bang's right hand man was, the fall, combined with his other injuries, was to his death.

Wrenching himself back into the apartment, the Moon Man collapsed on the floor. Minutes were all he had before people showed up, having heard the gunfire. The Moon Man staggered to his feet and furiously scanned the apartment for any clue that might present itself.

Fifteen seconds, thirty seconds, fifty-six seconds. Nothing. There wasn't any time left. The Moon Man had to leave. He hurried to the door and opened it. There were noises coming up the staircase. He would have unwanted company momentarily. The Moon Man ached excruciatingly. Another man was dead. For what? Not a bloody, damned thing.

Stephen rolled the La Salle into the darkened alley. He parked the car where no one was around and removed the key from the ignition. This key was the last thing he had seen exiting Bloom's apartment, sitting in an unused ashtray by the door. After he snuck to the main floor to change into his civilian clothes, Stephen located the Cadillac that matched the key in front of the building and sped off.

The detective lifted his shirt to check for cracked ribs. The bruises were darkening but he seemed to be fracture free. Stephen laid his head back for a few minutes to rest a little. When he had calmed himself sufficiently, he opened the glove compartment to look for anything that might suggest the arsonist's identity. He didn't have to look too far.

Stephen pulled out a piece of paper with a phone number at the top. Underneath it was the address of 'Petersen Cigars and More' with a time written beside it corresponding with the time the fire had started. This was followed by the name 'Artie Gold' and a question mark. The note was probably written before Bloom had decided on which 'witness' to use. The written text below that info was similar but in a different pen color, signifying that it was added at a later time than the first blurb. This time it read, "Lang Haberdashery – April twenty-ninth – 11:00 – Josh Weber".

Today was April twenty-ninth. It was ten to 11:00 pm right now. Stephen's foot slammed down on the accelerator before he even placed the key back into the ignition. It took him ten minutes to arrive one block down from Lang Haberdashery. Not wanting to explain driving a mobster's Cadillac, Stephen walked the rest of the way in throbbing discomfort.

The flames flickered high into the sky. It was too late. The firebug had struck again. The heat that came off the small single-unit building made it impossible to approach. He would have to wait until the blaze died down, which would be after the fire and police departments showed up.

Lieutenant McEwen lit a cigar as he watched the burning shop lose its intensity. A few of his men stood around, waiting for orders that wouldn't come until the firemen tended to the flames. McEwen strolled over to Stephen who was sitting on the curb of Miller's Road. The darkness permeated by the flickering light helped disguise the forming bruises on Stephen's neck and cheek. McEwen wasn't staring at him, anyway, as he took in the fiery destruction.

"How did you get to be first on the scene, Stephen?"

"Stumbled across it as I was getting in my rehabilitation exercise."

"This is a long walk from your place."

"I'm eager to get back to work. I may be overdoing it."

"Not the smartest move."

"So your daughter keeps telling me... about everything," Stephen quipped. He got the intended smirk out of his friend.

"See anything suspicious when you arrived?"

"Sorry, Gil," Stephen answered with remorse. There was nothing he could mention without a further conversation as to how he acquired the information. There really wasn't much more to say. After twenty more minutes of watching the fire department tackle a catastrophe that only time would be able to truly arrest, McEwen ordered one of his men to drive Stephen home, an action that Stephen didn't protest. He was dead on his feet and this night was going to last a lot longer for Great City's Finest.

Sue scolded Stephen for what seemed like half the morning. The Moon Man was something she understood, even supported, but not at the expense of Stephen's life. He was pushing himself far past what the normal human body should endure. The scolding eventually turned to passion, a smoldering embrace replacing the yelling and pleading, until Angel showed up.

"What's the plan, boss?" asked Angel, helping himself to the contents of Stephen's fridge. Usually they would meet at Angel's place, but Sue believed that Stephen needed to remain at home to heal.

"We only have two avenues to pursue as far as I can see," Stephen deduced, trying to sit up. Sue's tender but firm grip on his shoulder prevented him from moving out of his horizontal position. "See if there is anything in the police report that will be filed later today is one. The other is tracking down a 'Mr. Joshua Weber'."

"Who's he?" Sue inquired.

"I'm betting he is going to be the witness for the haberdashery fire. Getting to him before he gives a statement will give us an upper hand. I need to find out where he lives and..."

"You're not going anywhere right now except to sleep," proclaimed the lieutenant's daughter as she held her lover down once again. "When the police report is drawn up, then you can play detective. As for Weber, you will be leaving that to Angel and me."

"Sue." Stephen could only get out the one word before he was greeted with a finger to his lips.

"This is not a 'but' moment, Stephen," she insisted. "We can confront this Mr. Weber just as well as you. It might even help that we don't have badges and civic responsibilities."

"Angel..." Stephen looked to his pal for back up.

"Sorry, boss," Ned spurted out with the remains of a bologna and tomato sandwich. "We've got this. Sue, we should probably head out."

"I have to use the lavatory first," she blushed. "Give me two seconds."

"Take a full five," Angel said with a smile as Sue ducked into the bathroom. Angel whispered to Stephen.

"Bloom's dead?"

"Yes," Stephen said with obvious remorse. "Sue doesn't have to know about Bloom."

"Not from my lips."

"You're a good man, Angel."

"Learned from the best," Ned responded. By the time Sue exited the washroom, Stephen had passed into dreamland.

Joshua Weber lived in a small house with his sister's family. He hadn't had full-time employment in over three months and had been relegated to babysitting his two nieces and two nephews to pay for his room and board. At eleven a.m., he was playing tag with the three oldest children outside while the baby slept on the front stoop. Josh was great with the kids but he needed to get back on his feet, get his own place. He was a clever man despite his crippled hand and had found a way to begin his trip back to self-sufficiency. He would be a witness to an event he had not actually seen. But he would not be paid until he gave the police his statement. And he couldn't do that until his sister Beth returned home from her job as a receptionist. In the end, it wouldn't matter anyway.

Seeing Sue and Angel approach, Weber suspected they might be trouble. He corralled his charges towards the front stoop and their sleeping sister. At first, the youngsters thought it was part of the game but they quickly recognized the tone of the situation.

"What do you want?" Weber asked rudely, trying to hide his crushed hand so as to seem more capable of offering up a good fight. With Angel as imposing as he was, nobody was buying Weber's bluff.

"Are you Joshua Weber?" Sue asked politely.

"I am. I asked what you wanted."

"We need to have a serious talk, Mr.Weber."

"About..?"

"The witness statement you gave to the police about the fire on Miller's Road."

"What... I... I didn't give a statement," Josh blurted in disbelief.

"Not yet," Sue said.

"That's how serious the talk is," added Angel with frightening effect. Josh's first instinct was to run but he couldn't leave the children. He was stuck. Good people aren't always adept at doing bad things.

"Mr. Bloom send you?"

"We're not mobsters," Sue declared.

"Can you wait until my sister gets back before you take me in?" Weber pleaded. "Otherwise, there isn't anyone to look after them."

"Not cops neither," Angel added. Weber was still scared no matter what category the bruiser fell into. "We do want to know anything you know about that fire."

"How do you mean?"

"We know all about Bloom. What else ya got?"

"I don't know." Weber's head started to swirl, aware that he needed to give this man something. "I was supposed to go in and say I saw the owner, Lang, leaving the shop minutes before it went up."

"Anything else?" Sue asked firmly.

"N-no," Weber stuttered. "That's all I know about the revenge job."

"Revenge?"

"Bloom said something to that effect when he was talking to his friend. They were walking away but they weren't out of earshot. Bloom mentioned that he felt his pain. I think the other fellow's name was Hyman."

"What did the friend look like?"

"Few inches shy of six feet. Big mane of dark hair."

"Sounds like our trench coat guy," Sue shared with Ned.

"Uh huh." Angel got right up close to Weber's face, putting a period on a statement that had already been driven home. "You won't be going to the police today, or any time soon." Josh Weber wouldn't.

Stephen navigated down the steps in front of the precinct carefully. The strain he put on his still tired body to get here was hardly worth the effort. McEwen informed him that his men had not found any kind of note. Broken window, two flaming vodka bottles, nothing else. Joseph Lang wasn't much more help. He was out of town visiting a friend on his birthday. The alibi was confirmed. It was good for Lang but didn't serve

"We need to have a serious talk, Mr. Weber."

Rudy Petersen's case any. And speak of the devil.

"Tell me there's some good news," Rudy hoped as he caught Stephen on the last step.

"Actually, a little worse. You have an alibi for last night?"

"Why? Was there another fire? Is that why they called me in to have a 'chat'?"

"Most probably. That alibi?"

"Home by myself all night reading Ellery Queen."

"That's not good."

"What should I do?" Rudy's face drained of most of its color.

"Tell the truth, pray, and leave the rest to me." Stephen put his hand on Rudy's shoulder then watched his sometimes friend march up the precinct steps. Stephen ambled a block before Angel's black roadster with Sue in the passenger side pulled up beside him. As they zoomed away, the trio compared notes.

After reporting his lack of news, Stephen took in the nuggets that his partners uncovered from Josh Weber.

"Hyman and revenge. Partial name and motive. That's twice as much as we had before."

"Now where to?" Angel inquired behind the wheel.

"Drive around a bit," Stephen instructed. "I need to think." The Moon Man's brain circled around the presumably related cases, trying to find a way into the inner circle of the whole mystery. Two fires started from outside by breaking windows and hurling in fuel and flames. Two stores – one for cigars, one for hats – in entirely different neighborhoods. Hmm, that didn't seem to go anywhere.

Unsuccessful with that line of thought, the Moon Man mulled over the only other aspects of the case he knew as certainties: the people involved. The victims: Rudy Petersen and Joseph Lang. The bad guys: Jules Popper's main man, Isaac Bloom, and Hyman somebody. Even the witnesses: Arthur Gold and Josh Weber. Did they have anything in common? It took a few minutes but when he came around to it, the connections seemed almost obvious. The suspects and the witnesses they employed were all Jewish. The victims were German. It was nearing April 1939 and things were volatile in Europe. There was talk of a great war. Nobody wanted that.

"We need to find a record of all Jewish immigrants from Germany, then spread out through the countries that border it," Stephen suggested.

"Pal," Angel sighed, "that smells like a lot of paperwork."

It was. Two weeks of sneaking requests to several municipal and federal agencies, seemingly endless runarounds, and avoiding anybody of consequence in the police department finding out – most importantly Stephen's dad and Sue's – led to one man who had the first name and attributes Stephen was looking for. Hyman Blumenthal.

The Moon Man waited an hour after the lights went out at 223 York Avenue before he moved out of his hiding place: a large, leafy tree in a park across the street. It was one a.m. as he went to the back door of the bungalow and picked the lock. Hyman was renting the house for a cheap sum. The door opened without a sound but a clink emerged from another part of the small house. Almost imperceptible but the Moon Man had caught it. Quickly checking the door, he noticed a nylon fishing line attached to it and slipping through a hole drilled in the wall. It was a makeshift alarm system. Odds are the line was connected to a tin can in Hyman's bedroom that would sound when the back door was opened. The renter knew he was not alone.

Realizing the element of surprise was gone, the Moon Man bolted through the house. The smell of turpentine reached him before he could reach Hyman. The first look he had of Hyman was that of him lighting a match. The minuscule flames slipped from the well coiffed man's fingers and onto the bed. Instantly, billows of flame separated Hyman and the Moon Man.

Hyman turned to perform a leaping somersault out the window. The Moon Man backtracked and raced out the back door. Hyman was running. Running away from the Moon Man again. He seemed to be always one step ahead of the modern-day Robin Hood – a Robin Hood who didn't see a penny to be gained by this entire ordeal. The reward would be the freedom of a man he knew to be innocent.

It was time to test out the last two weeks of rehabilitation.

The Moon Man began to jog. Feeling aches but no stabbing pains, he sped into a sprint. He hadn't pushed himself to this extreme in months. It felt bad but it also felt really good. The thigh felt like it was all one muscle, not two separated by a ghost splinter. The Moon Man gave it everything he had. Slowly he was gaining on Hyman. It might take a few blocks but at this rate, he would catch up to him. That was a fact... until he heard the gunshot.

The Moon Man's first instinct was to duck, assuming that Hyman was shooting at him. Then he realized the shot had been fired from behind instead of in front of him. Turning around, the Moon Man saw the one person he didn't want to see: his nemesis and friend, Gil McEwen.

"Don't move!" McEwen screamed as he pointed his firearm directly at the Moon Man. The warning shot that he had fired was still smoking out of the muzzle in the cold night. "I can't believe it. I would never have figured you for these fires. It's not your usual M.O. But seeing is believing."

Over the detective's shoulder, Hyman's rented house was in flames. The Moon Man didn't know what had brought McEwen to the locale, but he knew that if he didn't continue after Hyman, he would lose him. Maybe forever.

"I won't move," The Moon Man said calmly, "But if you want to save the child that is still in the yard of that burning house, you need to hurry." McEwen glanced back but didn't want to take his eyes off the Moon Man. He didn't believe the villain in the reflective helmet but the lieutenant couldn't take the chance. McEwen paused, swore, then darted back towards the house and the supposed endangered child.

Once McEwen had gone, the Moon Man took off in the other direction. He hoped that his friend would be okay, hence why he told him that the child was outside the bungalow and not in it. The Moon Man couldn't worry about the fire. The man who was setting them was still out there. He prayed that he wasn't too late to pick up his trail again.

The Moon Man followed the invisible line that Hyman appeared to be heading down. From several short detours to possible hiding places, he kept moving forward. If he stopped, the trail would die for sure. Like a shark. It always had to keep moving. But this shark was faster and probably fiercer. And it had gotten away.

McEwen was on his fifth cup of coffee when Stephen ambled into the squad room. The elder cop was happy to see that his friend was getting around like normal again. Stephen was a good officer, a good detective, and Gil was glad to have him back on the job.

"I can't call you Sir Limpsalot anymore," McEwen joked.

"You can but you'll get a kick in the ass if you do. You look tired. Long night?" Stephen knew very well what McEwen had been up to. He had almost caught the Moon Man then attended to a burning building. The lieutenant spilled all the details about the early morning incident. He had searched for the child and even went into the flaming house when the fire department arrived but there was no minor to be found. McEwen hated that he had been duped. It ate through him worse than the coffee was doing to his stomach lining.

"What led you to that house in the first place?" Stephen nudged.

"Got a call of a Moon Man sighting in the nearby park," Gil burped out. "I'm thinking he's behind these fires. We need to find the renter of the house... a Mr. Hyman Blumenthal. Find out what makes him a target for the Moon Man."

Stephen had been spotted on a stakeout. His leg might have mostly healed, but his vigilante work was rusty.

"If the arsonist is the Moon Man, then that makes Rudy Petersen innocent," Stephen proposed.

"Unless he is the Moon Man," McEwen pondered. "Let's go visit Mr. Petersen."

"I was... home, by myself," Rudy told McEwen, giving a similarly sparse alibi as the Lang Haberdashery fire.

"You really should get out more," McEwen jabbed.

Stephen could clear Rudy by proving that Hyman Blumenthal was the Great City Arsonist. But he also needed to stop the firebug. It seemed better for the moment that McEwen's attention was still on Rudy; that made the Moon Man's task of tracking down Blumenthal unimpeded and less difficult.

"Wait, I did go outside for a cigar and some fresh air late last night," Rudy amended. "My next door neighbor, Mal Schweitz, can vouch for me. He was coming in late from working security at the nightclub he works at." Stephen's luck was just as lousy as it had been for the last few months. At least, Rudy wouldn't be considered as the only possible suspect for the fires. His court case started in a week. Reasonable doubt had just entered the picture.

After ten more minutes of interrogating Rudy, McEwen and Stephen got in the lieutenant's car. The rest of the afternoon was spent scouring the city for Hyman Blumenthal, their latest witness. The two detectives checked with the real arsonist's former neighbors, community outreach centers, homeless shelters, and every police precinct in a five-mile radius. They came up empty-handed. Should the police pick up Hyman and discover that he was the responsible scoundrel, that would be fine by the Moon Man. However, that didn't seem likely and he couldn't tell McEwen what he had learned from his unsanctioned adventures. Stephen could only use that information during his own nightly escapades. The Moon Man was the only one who could close this case.

Stephen had been holding off doing what he needed to do next. But there was no more stalling it. The Moon Man had to visit the king of the Jewish mob: Jules "Pop Bang" Popper.

Since everything had been so problematic thus far, Stephen was flabbergasted that all the Moon Man had to do to talk to Pop Bang was simply walk in the front door. Sure, he was flanked by four large bodyguards upon entering the mob boss's inner sanctum but the mansion itself was air tight with so many security precautions and personnel, that there wasn't any other option. The Moon Man had been prepared to come in with a gun in each hand, aimed at anyone that looked at him funny, shooting anyone who didn't. Life throws curve balls sometimes.

"Mr. Popper," the Moon Man started, one gun on the boss, the second on his closest bodyguard, "no one gets hurt if I get a few answers."

"Answers, huh?" Pop Bang repeated. The mouse-like man in the robe a size too large for him repositioned himself on his large, comfortable chair, mulling over the suggestion. The Moon Man had never met Jules Popper before and he expected someone a little – heck, a lot – more intimidating. Popper stood up and walked over to the book case at the back of his home library. The Moon Man kept his forty-five on him. He followed the short man slowly, suspicious that a book was in actuality a secret lever for an even more secret escape passage. The bodyguards took one step for every one of the Moon Man's.

Popper pulled out a book and returned to stand before the muzzle of the automatic as he calmly opened up the old publication. It was a book of Jewish proverbs.

" 'Listen to your enemy, for God is talking.' " Popper closed the book and stared up at the reflective dome whose inhabitant was assuredly peering back. "You may think you are a hot brisket, your reputation and all, but you have now taken the role of my enemy. And as your enemy, you should listen to what I am about to say."

The Moon Man started to fidget slightly. He sensed the bodyguards inching closer though they didn't make a sound. The vigilante couldn't move forward without pushing his firearm into Pop Bang's face, an act that would surely cause the large men to rush him. Popper picked at his teeth with his long fingernail before resuming his speech.

"Unless you walk right back out the door you came through in mere moments, I will enact my right as God and end your life."

The Moon Man rethought his previous assessment about the mob boss's intimidation. Firming up his grip on his forty-five, he thought, after being on the receiving end of a cold speech like that, most men would have already been long gone. However, there was still an arsonist out there who might kill someone with his next set fire. And he was the Moon Man.

The first bullet caught the closest bodyguard in the shoulder, spinning the man entirely around because of the proximity. The Moon Man pivoted on his left heel while thrusting his body backwards against one of the most powerful men in Great City's underworld. The cracking of Pop Bang's nose coincided with the shattering of the next closest bodyguard's kneecap. In a flash, the only blond-haired gangster in the room was rolling on the floor in agony.

The two uninjured bodyguards pulled out Steyr-Hahns and unloaded their contents. As the Moon Man toppled over the reclining chair with Popper, one of the bullets cracked against his Argus helmet. Luckily, it ricocheted to the left, lodging itself into a billiards table at the other end of the large room. The remainder of the flying bullets dug into the chair, shattering wood and spraying goose feathers.

Not wanting to blindly murder their employer, the shooting ceased. The Moon Man jumped up from behind the chair, towing Popper with him. The forty-five was pressed against the mouse's temple as he acted as a disproportionate shield for the vigilante.

"I don't want to kill him," the Moon Man seethed, pretending that he would take the small man's life to protect his own, "but I will if I have to." It was a bluff he hoped the bodyguards would fall for. They did. Whereas Popper did not care if the Moon Man was telling the truth.

"Put many holes into this man," Popper demanded coolly, "even if you have to put them through me first."

The two bodyguards glanced at each other with uncertainty as the howls of their compatriots filled the sanctum. Blood poured down Popper's face and off his chin. His armed henchmen knew by the look in his eyes that he wasn't kidding. They raised their firearms.

The Moon Man sprinted across the room while bullets fired around Popper. A smearing of blood coated the air behind the mob boss as ammunition clipped his ear in half and tore a finger apart at the middle knuckle. The Moon Man jumped behind a couch near the pool table as a piece of lead pierced a hole through his cloak.

The Moon Man laid flat on his back as bullets tore through the sofa's fabric. He opened the Argus helmet then lifted it off his head. With the crack in it, he was never going to get a good shot off. Now he was able to place his head right up against the floor and peer under his hiding place. Two shots were all it took to drop the blasting bodyguards, a bullet per each left ankle. As he stood up, the Moon Man fired at the chandelier, shattering lights and causing it to short out. Darkness fell over the recreation room that had served as the O.K. Corral. Now the advantage was his. Swiftly he put the Argus globe over his head again.

"Fire at anything," Pop Bang's voice echoed through the silence of uncertainty. The bodyguards were reluctant to discharge their weapons. Frustrated, the mouse felt his way over to the front door where there was a rifle rack. If his men wouldn't kill this nuisance, he would have to do it. It gave Popper a thrill of anticipation. The man had murdered forty-nine in his life. He was about to crack the half-century mark. Or so he thought.

"That is my gun in your mouth," the Moon Man whispered as not to give away his position. He knew that the bodyguards' night vision hadn't adjusted yet. The Moon Man backed Popper to the other end of the room, avoiding the obstacles on the ground. The metal clinked against the mob boss's teeth, notching away at his bravado as they connected. "I know you're a tough guy. I just need to know one thing. Where is Hyman Blumenthal hiding? Your men can't hear us from over here so they'll never know you gave up the information. Then I'll leave. Talk to me. My patience is at its limit."

The muzzle slid out of the crime lord's mouth at a snail's pace. When it was completely out, Popper cleared his throat and began to talk in a hoarse voice.

"He's in the wind."

"Don't tell me you don't know where he is!" The Moon Man pressed the gun against Popper's broken nose. He could tell that the mobster was weighing his pride over his life. It was a difficult decision for him. The sound of blood dripping on the ground from Popper's nose, ear, and dangling finger was a ticking clock. The possibility of the mobster passing out from blood loss loomed.

"I'm not going to kill you," the Moon Man stated in a whisper, which seemed like an odd intimidation tactic to Pop Bang. "I am going to blow off your cojones and let you live your life without them. No more 'Pop'

"That is my gun in your mouth..."

with the ladies. No more 'Bang'."

"Tonight he will be at a warehouse on Kennedy," Popper gave up. The pride was gone from his speech. "It's his grand finale. Now get out of my home."

"There are several warehouses on Kennedy."

"That's all I know," the mobster claimed. "That is the truth."

"Why is he burning down these buildings?"

"I owe his uncle from a long time ago. That's why I'm helping him with the witnesses. As to why he does what he does, you'll have to ask him that." Silence once again filled the gigantic room. After thirty seconds, Popper felt the need to replace it with his soft words again.

"I will kill you." Those words were not to be heard. The Moon Man was gone.

Sue McEwen had just brewed a cup of tea when she heard a knock on her window. The pounding code was a familiar one so she walked out into the backyard as the starry sky twinkled above her head. The always frightening blankness of the Moon Man's helmet greeted her. It was pristine, without a crack. The Moon Man had briefly stopped by Angel's place to grab a replacement and commandeer the assistance of his friend. He only accomplished one.

"Where's Angel?" the Moon Man said, having no time for pleasantries.

"I have no idea," answered Sue, detecting the desperation in her boyfriend's voice. "What's wrong?"

"Hyman is going to strike tonight. It's a warehouse on Kennedy. I made a few calls and have it narrowed down to two that are owned by Germans. I needed Angel for backup but there isn't time to find him."

"I'll come with you."

"No," the Moon Man forbade. "It's too dangerous. Look for him anywhere you can think of. If you find him, let him know where I've gone."

"Okay." Sue wasn't happy that Stephen was going alone. Sure, he had handled many horrible and dangerous situations on his own before but she never ceased to worry.

The Moon Man turned to leave but Sue touched his arm, creating an emotional tether to her. The orb rotated and she knew that they were peering at each other with love and tenderness. Nothing needed to be said.

Sue gathered her purse and keys from the kitchen then headed to her car. She racked her brain as she went through every location she thought Ned would visit on a Friday night. They were all bars. Sue sat in the driver's seat as she checked to make sure she had her revolver with her. The second knocking tonight scared the heck out of her. The fear subsided at the visage of her father motioning for her to roll down the window.

"Isn't it rather late to be heading out?" Lieutenant McEwen said to his daughter, more as an accusation then a question.

"I'm just going to Stephen's for awhile." Sue knew that might disappoint her father, visiting her boyfriend at this time, but it was the first lie that came to mind.

"You should have called him first," advised McEwen. "He's not home. I was just there."

"What did you need him for, Dad?"

"We got a tip about the whereabouts of a man that I think might be involved in the fires with the Moon Man. I wanted Stephen to come help me bring him in. But he ain't at home and he's not with you so forget it. I can't go hunting around the city for him."

Sue exited her car since her excuse was obliterated. Her father walked her back to the front door and asked, "If he drops by later, where should I tell him to meet you?"

"Good idea," McEwen nodded. "Tell him a 'Hyman Blumenthal' was spotted. He should look for my car on Kennedy. It will be parked outside one of the warehouses. Good night, baby."

McEwen kissed his daughter on the forehead then waited for her to close and lock the door before he left. Sue rested her back against the inside of the door. There was no time to look for Angel. Sue had no choice. She had to warn Stephen that he was going to have company.

The Moon Man slid down a rope he had lowered from the ceiling of a warehouse owned by Zimmerman's Appliances. The place was quite dark as the only light source at the moment was from the moon shining through the horizontal rectangle windows at the top of the fifty-foot-tall room. With a tap, his shoes connected with the concrete that paved the floor of the massive warehouse. If this was the establishment that Hyman Blumenthal planned to burn down, the man had his work cut out for him. Sure there were hundreds of unvarnished crates in the building but the piles of wood boxes had large gaps in between them, probably so loading trucks could drive down the aisles. Logic drifted towards his having the wrong warehouse. Hyman would have to go to each towering pile of crates and separately light them on fire to level the building. Unless he connected each one with some kind of accelerant: like gunpowder.

The Moon Man got down on one knee and sifted the black granules in his glove. He had almost missed the trail in the dark. The Moon Man peered around and made out a couple of other thick lines leading from one stack of large crates to another. This was it. However, the warehouse was massive. The crates created the high walls of a maze that went on for two blocks of real estate. If he was going to stop the Great City Arsonist from finishing his blazing masterpiece, he was going to need all his speed and most of his luck.

Scanning left and right as he aimlessly weaved through the labyrinth, the Moon Man glimpsed more and more gunpowder trails. Hyman had been at this for awhile. Odds were that the igniting match would be struck sometime soon.

Click. The Moon Man stopped. The noise originated from the direction he had just navigated through. Clinging to the side of a crate stack, the Moon Man pulled out his forty-five and listened. Click. Footsteps – slow – heading in his direction. Either Hyman knew that the Moon Man was here and was coming after him or the firebug was about to be in for a big surprise. Click. Click. Click.

The footsteps were almost upon him. With the extremely limited lunar light floating in, the Moon Man witnessed a shadow emerging down the closest alley. He counted backwards in his head. Three. Two. One. The Moon Man whipped around the crates and raised his gun right at Hyman's forehead.

Unless Hyman had grown light brown hair and remolded his face into a heart shape, the Moon Man had just aimed his firearm at the love of his life.

"Sue?" the Moon Man whispered harshly. "I told you not to come here. How did you even know where to look?"

"Zimmerman is a German name and the wall ladder to the roof made it the best guess," Sue stated succinctly, pointing at the still dangling rope on which they both shimmied down. "When I saw that rope, I knew I was at the right place."

"You need to get out of here. This is too dangerous and it is about to get – "

"I had to warn you," Sue interrupted. "My father is searching Kennedy to find Hyman."

"A patrol car must have spotted him. Your father gave each man a detailed description of him provided by Hyman's landlord. How many men did your dad bring with him?"

"I snuck past him and three others. They were talking about splitting up so I assume that there was only them."

"Okay." The Moon Man took a moment to think. "There are a lot of warehouses on this strip so as long as I can nab Hyman before he sets a fire, I should be able to gift wrap him for the lieutenant and disappear before I'm spotted."

No sooner did the words leave the Moon Man's mouth, when the unmistakable woosh of a fire birthed into life at the far end of the warehouse.

"Dammit!" the Moon Man cried as things instantly got more complicated. "Do you think you can climb back up the rope?"

"Yes," Sue said as she hugged the Moon Man. "Don't worry about me. Go get him."

With that, they sprinted in opposite directions. The Moon Man darted towards the life-threatening blaze. The fire was contained to one tower of crates but that was sure to be temporary. Just like that, a second stack caught fire, wood sizzling and crackling as he was only yards away.

One corner. Then another. The Moon Man winded through as the temperature rose with each footfall until finally he was in the middle of Hyman's handiwork. With his back turned to the Moon Man, Hyman frantically collected his supplies. The Moon Man had a perfect chance to take him unaware. Dashing between two flaming towers, he was almost upon Hyman when a small explosion rocked him off his feet. The blast did the same to Hyman, causing him to topple over.

Sue was halfway up the rope when she heard the eruption and caught a glint of her lover's Argus helmet near the site. She couldn't leave him now. Rope burn seared her hands as she slid down to the ground. Ignoring the pain, Sue raced towards the flickering lights across the obstacle littered expanse.

It took only a minute for her to race down the aisles and around the crates, noticing portions of crate stacks catching fire the closer she got. Finally, when she arrived at the site, she was relieved to see that the Moon Man was alive. He was locked in a struggle with the terrible arsonist. Analyzing the situation, Sue figured she could tip the scales in the Moon Man's favor if she could only find a way to get behind the bad guy and knock him out with something. Wait, where was the Moon Man's gun? The term 'pistol-whipped' came to mind, and Sue became occupied with the task of finding the weapon. Maneuvering around the flaming partitions of crates, she was able to locate the gun. It was lying by the warehouse's outlying wall... near the open door... right beside the well polished shoe of Lieutenant Gil McEwen.

"Hands up, both of you," Sue's father howled. The lieutenant was joined by the three uniformed officers as they all pulled their pistols on the men they thought responsible for the raging inferno. "Walk to us slowly. No funny stuff."

Sue jumped behind a untorched crate before her father could spot her.

Hyman Blumenthal watched with disbelief as his escape route was blocked by the four coppers. Unlike his other crimes, this one spelled his finish. But he had no intentions of being captured alive. Hyman was going another way.

Before Lieutenant McEwen could repeat his orders, Hyman dashed behind several blazing towers and ran deeper into the warehouse. Everybody was shocked, but the Moon Man didn't let it stop him from reacting. He stormed after him while the silent pistols of the GCPD followed his progression until he, too, disappeared.

"White, go get reinforcements and the fire boys," addressed McEwen. "You two..." McEwen and his other two men followed his outstretched index finger and headed between two burning stacks.

"And men," McEwen continued as they marched forwarded, covering their faces from the licking flames, "do whatever is necessary to bring them in."

Sue knew what that meant. It wasn't as cold-blooded as it sounded. Her father wasn't a killer. But in a situation like this, a bullet might be the only option and a policeman's life was worth more than a perceived thug's.

Hyman kicked some flaming boards to the floor behind. Though he blocked the projectiles easily with his forearm, the Moon Man's cloak caught fire. He struggled to remove it and left it lying on the ground. In this environment, a loose, flapping fabric was not a great fashion accessory.

"Halt." The police were behind the Moon Man, glimpsing him then losing him in alternating seconds. Hyman was doing the same to him, running a good twenty paces ahead. The fire was spreading. The heat was climbing. Emotions were flaring up as well as a shot rang out from one of the policeman's guns. Accident or not, there were too many variables present that could mark the end of the Moon Man.

A wooden staircase leading up three flights, came into view. It led to a loft, presumably where a foreman did his supervising and paperwork. Hyman took the stairs two at a time hoping, the loft led to an alternative exit. He couldn't correct his mistake in time. The Moon Man was up the same staircase blocking the doorway. The tall stage was open but jumping the thirty feet back down to the main floor would end with a broken ankle or on a bonfire. Hyman spotted a crowbar on the floor and picked it up despite its near scorching temperature.

"Out of my way," demanded Hyman, waving his weapon over his head. The Moon Man revealed his thirty-eight.

"Just drop it, Hyman."

"I don't think I will," Hyman replied. In the last few weeks, the Moon Man had been challenged by cool customers, who seemed like they would die rather than back down. Hyman was the same but different. He wasn't about pride or ego. Hyman's defiance was of a sadder substance. The Moon Man couldn't believe it but he suddenly felt pity for the man.

"Drop your weapons," McEwen called out from the main floor below. If the arsonist and the vigilante heard him, they didn't show it. McEwen turned to his men. "Let's go. If one of them so much as turns our way, fire."

Sue panicked. She was hiding right behind the police officers but they were too preoccupied to notice. There had to be something she could do to stop them. She was out of time. Sue couldn't think of anything, so circumstance took over.

A burning tower collapsed and smashed into the one beside it. Large sections of shattered wood and pieces of refrigeration units rained down on Sue, knocking her to the ground and trapping her in rubble. Still conscious, she screamed for help and McEwen recognized her voice. He and his men ran to the ramshackle prison.

"Susan!" McEwen yelled. "Are you injured?"

"I don't... no, not bad. But I can't... I'm pinned."

Lieutenant McEwen looked up at the nine feet of precariously balanced materials randomly arranged over his daughter. Some of them were on fire but not close enough to burn her. McEwen and his men couldn't simply throw off the components of the prison from the top down. It was a life-or-death game of Pick-up Sticks with his daughter's life in the balance.

The standoff devolved into a staring match. Hyman was willing to die but not drop the crowbar. The Moon Man didn't want to shoot him but he wasn't going to let him escape either. The two opponents breathed heavily as the air filled with more smoke. The far end of the warehouse was completely engulfed. It was only a matter of minutes before that hell took over the entire building. The Moon Man didn't know how long he had left to play this game. He was just relieved that Sue had made it out safely over ten minutes ago.

"What do you see as the next step here?" asked the Moon Man, hoping that Hyman might spark an idea in him as to how to conclude the situation. McEwen was going to show up any second and take the decision out of his hands.

"Take my life if you want," Hyman answered, with his heavy Yiddish accent. "I am done with it. That is what the Germans paid you for, anyway."

"I don't work for any Germans. I don't work for anyone."

Hyman looked perplexed, like a man who thought he knew the end to a movie and was surprised by the twist.

"Then why have you been following me?"

"You've been setting fires," the Moon Man said. A small explosion went off in the distance. More police officers and the fire department would be here soon.

"You do not work for the police?"

"No."

"Then who are you?"

"If you asked the police, they wouldn't give me a positive evaluation."

"You are what they would consider a bad guy, a villain?"

"Pretty much."

"Why do you care about what I do then?"

"I'll answer that if you answer a question for me first." This was crazy. It was Armageddon in the warehouse and they were having a conversation on personal philosophies. The curiosity in the Moon Man was piqued, though, as it was now obvious to him that this wasn't a run-of-the-mill mob thug or thrill-seeking arsonist. "What's your real reason behind setting the fires?"

"It's a long story."

"Give me the short version."

Hyman laughed briefly then sat down on a wooden chair, placing the crowbar on his lap. He was never leaving this place. It was his funeral pyre.

"I lived in Germany up until a few months ago. Do you know what is going on in Germany?"

"I hear it's very volatile. Some guy named Hitler is running the country and not with an open hand."

"It amazes me," Hyman sighed, "that even a villain like you could know this and still the world does nothing."

"It isn't our business to interfere in another nation's politics."

"It never is, is it? Until it affects someone you love."

Anderson, the sergeant that McEwen believed to have the most logical mind of the three, stood back and directed as to how to take apart the haphazard structure without allowing it to collapse. Each discarded material was a pulse pounding episode that took a year off of the lieutenant's life. Sweat poured down the men's faces as the heat reached the nineties. There was a real risk that his men could collapse at any time.

"What were you doing here?" McEwen asked his daughter, unable to let his parental duty of scrutiny fall to the wayside like one of the blackened boards.

"When you left, I looked out my window and saw the Moon Man following you in a car. I had to warn you." Sue had been waiting for the question. She felt this answer would not only give her a reason for being there but also insert some doubt that the Moon Man was a co-conspirator of the fire-bug.

"We're going to talk about this later, Missy," scolded McEwen, hurling another piece of debris off of the heap. Sue smiled at the concept of 'later'.

"I will, uh, what do you say... Oh! I will paint you a portrait." Hyman looked pained at remembering the past. "The night was November ninth of last year. My people, the Jewish people, had been oppressed for years before then. We were humiliated, sometimes beaten, sometimes thrown out of the country. The Germans who followed that evil little failure of a painter believed they were superior to everyone else, most especially the Jews. They thought they could do anything they wanted to us, this master race, and it got worse every day."

Hyman broke off for a second and it looked like he was about to cry. After composing himself, he went on, his voice faltering.

"Then that night... the ninth. Think about if hell came to Earth. A chaos that seemed impossible... impossible that a massive group of people could be this cruel and... and... demonic. The 'true' Germans took to the streets with pickaxes, sledgehammers, brandishing anything you could dream of with one aim; to destroy all the Jewish establishments they could find. This 'superior' race ransacked towns and villages. They beat people and burned down shops." Hyman paused. "They burned down shops... even if there were people inside. Even if they heard the screams."

Hyman stood up and strangled the crowbar in his tight fists. The Moon Man noticed that the staircase they had climbed up was on fire. It was time to leave. But the sobbing Jewish man, the man with the still immaculate black hair, wasn't finished giving his own eulogy.

"My parents owned a bicycle shop. It was a beautiful, wood-carved building. They were even more beautiful. Beauty can't break down a door when the German's prop steel bars between it and the ground. Beauty can't jump through a window when it is covered in burning tar."

"My father was a national hero. He saved five children in a flood when he was younger. While my parents were dying, the townsfolk called him a devil and told him he would be happy in his devil's hell. " Hyman's face twisted into that of a wounded animal. "They called him a villain when he was the kindest, most generous and helpful man I knew! Sometimes I think the words killed him before the flames. You can't possibly know the pain it caused him to be pronounced as a 'bad' man when everything he did was on the side of 'good'."

The Moon Man scanned around to find a way to escape the inferno when he spotted McEwen carrying Sue in his arms. The two adversaries locked eyes for a second. The Moon Man could feel the animosity that the lieutenant had for him. McEwen quickly hauled his daughter away with the other policemen behind him.

"We have to get out of here," warned the Moon Man but he was talking to a man that could only hear himself.

"They called this man-made devastation 'Kristallnacht'. The Night of Broken Glass. Two weeks later, I was on a boat to America. Before I left, however, I learned the names of the men who burned my parents to death. My cousin, who was hiding, saw the four men and knew three of them. Their last names were Petersen, Lang, and Zimmerman."

Those were the names of the shop owners that Hyman had targeted.

"Were the men whose shops you burned to the ground, the men you tried to frame for those fires, related to the ones who killed your parents?" the Moon Man asked. He spotted the rope he had dropped down from the ceiling swaying in the heat swirls, flames eating at the bottom and swallowing it fast.

"Does it matter?" Hyman said with blank eyes. "But I never killed anyone. I waited until everyone had left the buildings. I'm not a monster like them."

"You preyed upon people simply because of their nationality. What kind of monster does that make you then?"

Hyman's face fell as he took in those words. His eyes soon settled on the preoccupied vigilante's pistol.

"If we jump on the crate there and both jump for my rope at the same time, we can climb up before the flames catch us. But we have to go right now otherwise –"

Suddenly Hyman swung the crowbar up and it hit the Moon Man's hand; his gun falling to the floor. Hyman scooped it up and pointed it at the vigilante, "Go."

Having no other recourse, the Moon Man turned and leaped onto a shaky structure of crates. Without stopping, he bounded over to grasp the rope. The hungry flames licked at the Moon Man's feet as he wrenched himself upward to the ceiling. Using the rafters, he swung along to the window he had originally climbed in. He then turned to witness the final moments of Hyman Blumenthal as he sauntered into the middle of his own personal hell.

The rain fell to the ground with the pounding of splattering eggs. Water was a welcome relief. The Moon Man had enough of its elemental counterpart to last him years. The deluge had started four days ago when Stephen finally was able to tell Rudy Petersen that he was no longer a suspect in the Great City Arsonist case.

With a sigh that was like a bell chiming the farewell of a younger life, Stephen brought his mind back to the present. He checked his pocket watch, squinting to see the time in the obscure light of the alley. There were three more minutes. He knew he wouldn't have to wait longer than that. The man he was expecting obsessed about being on time.

A gray mist collected around the Moon Man's feet. He was tired of the grays of the world, tired of the ambiguities. He wanted to go back to black and white. Rob from the rich; give to the poor. It was an absolute. He needed an absolute after the events in the warehouse... and there was nobody that oozed absolute evil like Jules Popper. By extension, that included Pop Bang's henchmen who did his dirty deeds in Great City. Like Armin Rosenburg, numbers runner, leg breaker. The man that was always right on time.

Rosenburg strolled into the alley at eleven-thirty p.m. on the dot. This was when and where he paid out the lost bets for the day – the Jewish mob's winnings were collected at eleven somewhere else. Two big lugs guarded the mouth of the alley so that nobody unwanted would come in during the proceedings. They didn't expect someone to have been waiting in the sewers for the last hour.

The Moon Man rose up slowly, his helmet appearing in front of Armin just like his name suggested. His forty-five lined up between the henchmen's eyes and he gleefully uttered, "Hi Armin, I need to make a withdrawal."

THE END

PHASES OF THE MOON

*I*t was an event that was a first in many regards. I am referring to the first annual PulpArk convention in Batesville, Arkansas that took place in May of 2011. It was the first time I had ever been to a convention as a writer and a panelist, instead of just a fan. It was also the first time I had ever been in the company of so many fellow writers, peers in the world of pulp fiction. The movement known as New Pulp was revealed here, and I felt (as I believe many others did) that we were at the relaunch of a kind of writing that had gone into a pseudo-hibernation over that last few decades. Sure, there have always been spikes of resurgence from time to time since the art form waned in the 1950s but with the emergence of new technologies like the iPad, Kindle, and other portable prose-reading devices, the action-packed tales are at their highest demand in the last half century. The "first", however, that is the reason I am writing both this essay and the Moon Man story in this anthology is my first meeting with the founder and Captain of Airship27, Ron Fortier.

All the creators that traveled to Arkansas for the convention shared quite a few meals and moments together during that weekend. A lot of it was the celebratory nature that takes over when people are on a "working" vacation with new friends. Some of it was still business. I had been familiar with Airship27 and after getting to know Ron, I really wanted to do something for not only his company but him in particular. I asked him if that was a possibility and amazingly (at least "amazingly" to me) he said "yes".

Now as to why I chose to write a Moon Man story. That decision was tangentially implanted in me over three decades ago. There were several characters that I loved when I was a kid and never knew their connection to the world of pulp fiction. These characters weren't developed in the golden era of pulp but they either were obvious influences on the pulp world, or were influenced themselves. Sherlock Holmes, Robin Hood, the Three Investigators, Scooby Doo, the Question. These nuggets of fiction from many a media were my favorites. So when I looked at Ron's list of characters about which he was interested in making anthologies, it only took the term "a true modern-day Robin Hood" under the Moon Man heading to make my decision for me.

The funny thing is, the story I decided to write didn't really focus on the pulp character's "rob from the rich, give to the poor" aspect. I saw something deeper, and ultimately more intriguing, in the character and his mythos. The Moon Man was a true dichotomy. He acted as a villain when in reality he was a hero. His alter ego served on the Great City Police Department while the vigilante side worked with disregard to the laws of the land. The Moon Man's greatest adversary was his best friend. These things were what I believed made this character great, and I was quite pleased with the outcome of the story I presented in these pages.

As far as "firsts" go, the writing of the Moon Man story and creating a chunk of his legend was one of pure joy; a first that I hope it is also not a last.

KEN JANSSENS - is a writer living in the extreme climates of Winnipeg, Manitoba, Canada. He is the creator and writer of the Aloha McCoy, Sherringford Bell, and Cerberus Clan stories for ProSe Productions. He has also been published in Pulp Empire Vol. 2.

In late 2011/early 2012, Ken's graphic novel *Caleb Elsewhere* will be published by ProSe Productions and his Sherlock Holmes comic book mini-series will hit the stands courtesy of Bluewater Productions.

BLACK MOON
by
Andrew Salmon

Ned 'Angel' Dargan tore his gaze off the full moon, the second of the month, the black moon, and spat into the turgid waters of Murder River. Worry was a digging claw in his gut. The Moon Man was late. Dargan had a nose for trouble and even the stink wafting off Murder River couldn't mask the scene of danger he'd picked up since he and the Moon Man had parted company at sundown.

Dargan, an ex-pugilist with no neck and a cauliflower ear, had been down and out in the gutter thanks to a bum arm keeping him out of the ring. Sick, dying of starvation, the Moon Man had lifted him up, nursed him back to health. Now Dargan dedicated himself to the Moon Man's cause – helping others brought low by the Depression. He was the Moon Man's ambassador, distributing the money his benefactor stole from those raking it in illegally and putting it in the hands of those who needed it the most. He did not do this for the tarnished honor that came with the job. And even though the happiness he brought to those in need – grateful citizens who had dubbed him the 'Angel' as they did not know his name – this was not his true motivation. No, he did it because the Moon Man needed it done. Dargan would gladly lay down his life to preserve that of his benefactor.

Which is why his ring-hardened fists clenched futilely as he awaited the Moon Man's return.

Gunfire erupted behind him.

Dargan whirled, eyes probing the darkness.

He was near Suicide's Leap which flanked the river road – a soaring precipice just past the wharf-houses, coal sheds and piers dotting the banks. The area was thick with trees.

A Thompson chattered. Shouts. Sticks and leaves crackled under numerous running feet.

Stray shots pinged off the rocks to Dargan's right. He crouched behind a skeletal shrub, unsure whether the shots were accidental or deliberately aimed in his direction.

The place was too hot for a pick up. Surely the Moon Man would realize that.

Dargan crouch-walked his squat frame towards the roadster and crawled behind the wheel. The starter growled.

The full moon broke through the blackening overcast sky, silvering the churning Murder River being hauled by the unseen hands of the current. Ghostly light winked off something just offshore.

The firing had stopped as quickly as it had begun. Voices echoed through the woods, calling excitedly, reaching Dargan faintly. They held a note of triumph.

Head cocked towards the trees, Dargan did not at first see the bobbing mass which had caught the moon's rays as it was yanked along. Then the moonlight hit the shiny object at the center of the drifting mass and the gleam caught in the corner of his eye.

He turned and gasped.

It was the Moon Man's unique Argus glass helmet that had gleamed in the night, a glittering sphere in the swirling black cloak floating on the surface.

Frantic, Dargan was momentarily torn between leaping into the river after his benefactor or putting the roadster into motion to follow the drifting form. He was halfway out of the car before realizing the current was too swift and he'd never catch up to the Moon Man.

An eddy pool lay a quarter mile ahead – the local kids fished it in the summer months.

The voices grew louder, more distinct. The gunmen drew near. Any second they would break out of the trees and see the automobile.

Dargan gunned the motor to life – hopeful the forest would play hell with the echo and buy him the time he needed to get back on the road running parallel to Murder River.

Time!

That water had to be like a million tiny daggers in the Moon Man's flesh. No man could survive long in that freezing bath.

The engine roared bringing shouts and the roadster churned tundra-like grass as it shot forward.

Dargan found the road without using the head lamps – did not turn them on at all so he could keep an eye on the receding form of the Moon Man. The roadster pulled slightly ahead of the drifting mass.

Jerking the wheel hard, he skidded off the road to the grassy embankment leading down to the eddy pool. He launched himself out of the auto, hopped the low guard rail and slid down the gentle slope to the river's edge. He darted his gaze upstream. If he was too late, and the Moon Man had passed this spot, there would be no saving him and his benefactor would freeze to death long before drifting out to sea.

There!

The mirrored glass deflected the moonlight. Dargan caught the glint.

The dome, in its black nest of cloak, was angling towards the eddy pool.

Dargan splashed knee-deep into the icy water, hands outstretched.

"Boss!" said Dargan. The relief in his voice evaporated. For as the figure drew closer, he saw dark splotches, black on black, in the feeble light of the moon's rays.

Blood!

"Boss!"

Dargan dove into the frigid water, fear gripping his heart as stinging cold burrowed through his skin. He did not feel the cold.

"Hang on, Boss!" Dargan urged as he thrashed towards the floating dome. "I'll have you out in a minute!"

At last he reached the dome. The water was shallow here and Dargan stood. The dome bobbed in the mass of sodden cloak.

"Can you stand, Boss?"

There was no reply.

Dargan took a fistful of the cloak and pulled it towards him. It came easily, gently. Dargan stood in water at his belly and yanked on the cloak which felt leaden in his hands.

"It's all right, Boss," soothed Dargan. "I've got you."

The glass sphere teetered in the folds of the cloak, then tumbled free. Dargan had to let go of the cloak in order to catch the falling globe. The cloak collapsed in a heap as the pugilist caught the mask before it hit the water. He tucked it under one arm and bent to help up his benefactor.

Pawing at the garment with one hand, Dargan's worst fears were realized.

It was just a cloak. There was no body, living or dead, in its folds.

It had been air trapped inside the inverted bowl that had kept the glass afloat. Enfolded by the cloak, the sphere had not tipped and filled with water.

Dargan's desperate gaze fixated on the blood stains dotting the garment and he groaned.

The Moon Man was gone!

Clouds engulfed the moon and Dargan's world was plunged into darkness.

Had Sue McEwen stepped out of the elevator on the fifth floor of Governor's Hospital blindfolded, she would have known she was on the right floor where Police Chief Peter Thatcher was recovering just by the loud shouting and baritone grumbling resounding along the corridor. Thatcher was in for observation for his ulcer. However a few days of imposed rest were not going to keep the crusty policeman from grousing from his hospital bed when there was work to be done.

Sue was young, beautiful, no more than twenty-two years old, brimming with youthful vigor. Light brown curls framed her heart-shaped face. As her trim figure started up the hallway she guessed the old chief was pontificating on the topic of the moment – the Moon Man.

The Moon Man was very much on her mind as well. It was her hope that Steve Thatcher would be there visiting his father as she had something to say to her fiancé. Stephen Thatcher, the man she loved and a Detective-Sergeant under Chief Thatcher's authority, was the very thief the police sought.

Stephen Thatcher was the Moon Man!

At the other end of the hall, at the nurse's station, a group of men talked animatedly. She recognized some of them as reporters for the Great City's dailies. They were unaware of her presence. A patrolman was stationed at the door to Thatcher's room. As she drew near, she heard the unmistakable gruff tones of her father, Gil McEwen. The reporters turned as McEwen's tone rose in pitch and they spotted her. A stampede began in her direction.

"I'm here to see the Chief," she explained breathlessly as the mob of reporters roiled up the corridor towards her.

The patrolman, a tall, rangy lad touched the brim of his peaked cap and knocked lightly on the door. Three taps, then two. "I recognize you, ma'am. You go right in. I'll handle this crowd."

The door latch clacked and Gil McEwen glared across the threshold. The frown on his lean, hard, weather-beaten face lifted when he saw his daughter but it returned a heartbeat later when he heard the stamp of worn shoe leather coming their way. He motioned Sue in with a quick jerk of his head.

Sue's heels clattered across the threshold. McEwen locked the door behind her as the reporters, restrained by the outstretched arms of the constable, hurled questions. McEwen edged past his daughter and went to stand at the foot of the bed upon which Chief Thatcher fumed, his unlit pipe clamped between his large teeth.

Sue's hesitant smile faded when she observed only two occupants in the room – her father and the Chief. Steve Thatcher was nowhere to be seen.

"Damn jackals!" McEwen blurted, running a gnarled hand through his iron gray hair. "Sue! By damn, have you seen Steve? We've got problems here."

"N-No, I haven't," she replied and a fist of ice closed around her heart. The chances he took as the Moon Man – "I thought he might be here. Did he drop in to see you this morning?" This last she directed at Chief Thatcher.

"Haven't seen hide nor hair of him since yesterday afternoon." In his sixties, Thatcher was a bit long in the waistband but his keen blue eyes blazed from his fleshy face in its tangle of curly hair as white as the hospital sheet around him. "We've got bigger fish to fry at the moment. Have you seen the papers?"

"I came right over. What's going on?"

Chief Thatcher thrust a wadded up morning edition of the Evening Standard at her.

Sue smoothed the sheet with her small, gloved hands and read:

HIGH SOCIETY HAS IT UP TO HERE WITH BUNGLING BLUESUITS!

It appears a group of well-to-do citizens have had enough of being stuck up by crooks and robbers. They have had enough of the ineptitude of Great City's flattest. They've put their wallets together and trucked in some private protection. That's right folks, Stalwart Security is on the job and the Moon Man and his ilk are on the run. In just a few short days, the Stalwart boys have racked up an impressive array of crimebusting daring-do and given our blueboys something to cry about.

Making your way about town, you may have noticed our well-dressed protectors at the bank, guarding our burg's wealth, or outside the factory, escorting the payroll. That's right, folks, Stalwart Security is making their presence known. You'll know them by the tuxedoes they wear topped with executioner's hoods. But don't be alarmed. The hangman's hood is for the crooks of Great City, not decent, upstanding citizens. Skin your eyes for them and be reassured.

If you will indulge me for a moment as I haul out my soapbox, it comes as no surprise that some of our wealthy citizens have forked over for their own Praetorian guard. You don't have to live in our fair town long to know that the police are unable to keep the peace. They've let the Moon Man run amok and it's a sad state of affairs these days. With everyone tightening their belts it seems a shame to be wasting taxpayers dollars on a bunch of blue-suited clods who can't get the job done.

More power to you, Stalwart Boys! Great City is confident you'll be able to clean up the mess...

Sue looked up from the paper, her brown eyes tinged with anguish. "Oh, Dad! This is terrible!"

Chief Thatcher's voice sounded suddenly old and frail from the bed. "That rag doesn't tell the whole story."

"What could possibly be worse?" Sue asked.

It pained Gil McEwen to see the old man suddenly burdened by the weight of his years. Gil loved the Chief and would walk through fire for him, but his inability to run the Moon Man to ground despite his best efforts smacked of failure, which was like acid in his gut. Now his failure was about to land square on the revered man's shoulders.

"By damn, I've put the Chief's head on the chopping block," Gil complained. "And I've given the department a black eye in the process! All because of that damn Moon Man! If I could just get my hands on him!"

"Stop that!" Thatcher wouldn't tolerate the self-recrimination in McEwen's tone.

Gil McEwen was the ace detective on the force. No perpetrator had ever escaped his long reach. He'd even gone overseas hunting his prey. The old chief knew this and was certain the veteran lieutenant would snare the Moon Man sooner rather than later. Not only was Gil McEwen an exemplary police officer, the lieutenant was also like a younger brother to the wily old chief who loved him dearly.

Thatcher went on. "I've committed more resources to the Moon Man investigation and we will get our man while there's still time. We'll put those Stalwart boys to shame in the process."

Sue gasped, "Still time – "

"Don't you see?" Gil explained. "The rich muckety-mucks are forcing our hand with this Stalwart crowd. Sutton was just in here giving the chief the business courtesy of the board of police commissioners. Incompetence! Black eye for the Department! Embarrassment! Shameful! The works!"

Thatcher held up a restraining hand. "So I took my lumps. What of it? All in the line of duty. We'll show up Stalwart with fine police work. We'll clean up this city. We'll bring the Moon Man to heel."

"By damn, we will!" McEwen's eyes blazed with admiration for his boss and mentor.

Sue had no doubt these men meant what they said and a chill ran down her spine. "But, Dad, what about Steve?"

"We'll need him for the job ahead," McEwen replied. "Make no mistake. Where has that kid got to? You say you haven't spoken to him today?"

Sue's breath caught and her father's heart broke at the worry he saw in her young eyes. "He was supposed to telephone me last night," she explained. "We'd agreed. I didn't hear from him. I telephoned over to his flat this morning and there was no answer. I guessed he'd come to see the Chief and here I am. Where is he, Dad?"

Thatcher took up the thread of the conversation. "That boy is always running off on his own. He's part bloodhound that one. Well, we can't wait on him any longer. There's too much to do and not a lot of time for the doing. Gil, when you get clear of the reporters outside, use the radio car you came in to call in at the station. If Steve hasn't reported for duty, send a prowl car to his address. Let's see action!"

After saying their goodbyes, Sue followed her father downstairs. The reporters dogged them to the elevator, hurling questions which the pair ignored. Both breathed heavy sighs of relief when the operator closed the doors on the demanding mob.

The station thrummed with activity. Sutton had read them the Riot Act and the men were fired up with the desire to prove themselves. Lieutenant Gil McEwen threw gasoline on that fire. He stood up on one of the desks and called for their attention.

"Listen up, men! We're bringing in the Moon Man and all his ilk! You get that? We're not gonna let a paid goon squad make suckers out of us.

You all know what's at stake. I'm not just talking about our jobs here – we all know they are on the line – I'm talking about our pride and self-respect. The citizens of Great City think we can't protect them. They're wrong! And we're going to prove it to them!"

A cheer rang up from the assembled officers and the organized chaos resumed with more gusto. McEwen barked orders and officers jumped. Gil checked with the Desk Sergeant but Ryan had nothing to report. He strode over to Phone Sergeant Garcia. "Get me Steve Thatcher," he growled.

"Sorry, Lieutenant, Detective Sergeant Thatcher hasn't reported in. Metcalf is also a no-show. They are the only two who didn't respond to the squad call."

"By damn!" McEwen strode to an idle desk phone and ran the number through the operator.

The connection was made but Steve Thatcher's phone rang and rang. He got the same result at the home of Robert Metcalf.

McEwen banged the handset down and turned to Sue. "Steve picked a strange time for a holiday. And where the hell is Metcalf? I'll send units."

Sue, consumed with worry for Steve, could see the quick action around her and took advantage of it. "Wait, Dad. The whole department is jumping through hoops and you can't spare the manpower. I don't know about this other fellow, but I'll go find Steve."

McEwen accepted his daughter's suggestion with thanks and Sue found herself legging it to her automobile a minute later.

Although Sue was tempted to break every traffic law in the book, Gil McEwen had taught his daughter better than that. To her, the car seemed to crawl as she made her way to the street where Steve Thatcher resided. After what seemed an eternity, Sue pulled in across the street and killed the engine.

Every manner of calamity flew through Sue's mind as she walked the short distance up the snowy street to Steve's building. Although they had declared their undying love for each other, she had had a hard time accepting the fact that her fiancé was the Moon Man. Although she had come to terms with it, part of her railed against the loss of the normal life she'd dreamed about since she was a little girl while another part of her was filled with dread at the thought of Steve going down in a storm of gunfire with her father's finger on the trigger.

"Dear Lord," she said under her breath as Steve's building loomed before her. "If anything has happened to Steve, I'd die!"

Her fears propelled her up the steps to the entrance of the three-story walk up. Steve Thatcher had the third floor of the narrow tenement.

The street door was unlocked and she shoved it open. As she started up the stairs, she plunged trembling, fumbling fingers into her handbag for the set of keys to Steve's place.

It wasn't the icy cold of winter air that hampered her efforts to slide the key into the front door lock. The lock clacked open. Call it women's intuition or the deep connection shared between the couple, but she knew something had happened to Steve. Something terrible. Fearing the worst, she gave the door a tentative nudge. It did not move.

Her fears got the better of her. She threw her body against the door, pounding on the panel with one small, tight fist.

"Steve!" she wailed. "Steve!"

Then she saw the blood seeping out under the door into the hall.

"No!"

She rammed her palms against the dark wood but the door barely budged. Something soft, bulky kept the door from opening. With the strength of a tigress she launched herself at the door and it scraped open. The mass blocking the entryway from the other side shifted and the door swung wide.

Lying hunched over in a pool of his own blood was Stephen Thatcher.

Sue gasped as she bent over him, avoiding the blood. In her panicked dive, she knocked the small hall table just inside the door and it fell over with a crash. The door swung lazily closed behind her as she determined if he still lived. Tears spilled down her cheeks when she found the steady pulse at his strong neck.

There was a trickle of blood at the nape of his neck. She gently smoothed back tufts of his brown hair to reveal a large goose egg behind his left ear. A ragged hole in the shoulder of his suit jacket revealed the deep wound of a bullet. She shucked the coat off that shoulder. The bullet had not lost itself inside of him or shattered bone but had burrowed a deep groove through the skin and muscles there. The wound had bled considerably through the makeshift bandage he'd fashioned from his tie, which had slipped exposing the wound and allowing the blood to flow freely. It had stopped now, but the evidence of the wound's severity pooled on the floor around the two lovers.

"Steve, darling, what have they done to you?"

The sound of Sue's voice seemed to revive the young man. His eyelids fluttered and one hand twitched.

"Hold on, Steve!" Sue breathed. "I'll call for an ambulance."

Steve Thatcher's voice was a harsh rasp. "N-No! No ambulance! Hit my... head... that's all."

"You've been shot!"

Steve shook his head as if to clear it and a wave of agony made him wince. He raised one tentative hand to the back of his head, then let it fall. The pain cleared his mind.

"Sue!" he blurted as his mind cleared. "Thank God you're here. Help me up. Got to clean the wound out."

Thatcher was struggling to rise as Sue spoke. Seeing there would be no reasoning with him, she added her strength to his and helped him to stand.

"I'm all right, Sue," he assured. "Really, I am."

They started down the hall towards the bathroom. He sat down on the edge of the tub. "I came here to clean the wound and stow the Moon Man's automatic but a stab of pain staggered me and I fell, whacking my head on that damn hall table. I must have blacked out."

"You could have bled to death!"

"No, the bleeding had mostly stopped before I fell."

"Why didn't you call from wherever you were?"

"I was out at the river. No phones. Even if there were I couldn't risk that. I don't want to get you mixed up with the Moon Man."

"I'm already mixed up with the Moon Man." Sue turned, bandages and ointment in hand. "What happened?"

Blood trickled down his arm to pool at his elbow. "Can we hold off on the third degree until I get cleaned up?"

"Yes, Steve. Of course," Sue acquiesced but he knew her well enough to know his reprieve was a temporary one at best.

He told Sue about the botched robbery attempt while she worked on the wound. Sue had wiped away most of the blood as he finished relating what had happened. "Stalwart Security goons appeared out of nowhere," he finished up his tale, "firing at anything that moved. I was hit, bleeding. Out there in the middle of nowhere, where was I going to hide? So I got out of that outfit and faded away into the night."

"What became of the robe? The mask?"

"They're gone, honey. Gone."

Sue McEwen could barely contain her relief. That image of a normal, quiet life appeared before her mind's eye and a future of infinite possibilities seemed suddenly attainable. But she said, "What are you going to do?"

"I don't know, Sue, honey. I honestly don't know."

"They started down the hall towards the bathroom."

"Maybe some good came out of this, Steve," Sue considered in the attempt to change the subject before she fell down on her knees and thanked the Lord for this turn of events. "These hired guns are not sworn law officers. It'll look bad for them with the people, if the papers report that these fellows are shooting at police officers. We can claim that you were out there on a tip and caught got in the crossfire."

Steve Thatcher shook his head. "We can't do that."

Frustrated, Sue doused a cotton swap with rubbing alcohol and worked it roughly around his injured shoulder. Her action pushed a long hiss past the rictus of pain stretching his lips. The track of the bullet was deep, about an inch long. It was going to require stitches. There was a sewing kit under the sink in the kitchen.

Sue McEwen went to fetch the kit without a word. She sat down beside him, opened the kit and prepared a needle and thread. She fixed him with her gaze, needle poised in one hand. She was never more beautiful to him than at that moment. "Why not?"

He wiped the last of the blood from the wound before saying, "Because I was shot by a cop."

It was just after eleven when Steve Thatcher and Sue McEwen strode, hand in hand, through the doors of the precinct house. Word was quickly spread up to Gil McEwen's office where the Lieutenant was coordinating efforts to apprehend the Moon Man. In fact, he was just about to hit the bricks and urged Steve and Sue to wait for him in the lobby.

Steve tried not to move his damaged arm as he and Sue shifted to one side to avoid the officers coming and going. Together the two lovers had crudely sterilised and stitched Steve's shoulder wound. Layers of tight gauze controlled the bleeding and a dark sports jacket was selected in the hopes of masking blood leakage should any occur.

Sue had not undertaken the work without insisting that Stalwart Security should be called to the carpet for reckless shooting. Steve had had to remind her that he was out there as the Moon Man and a probe into how he came to be shot was asking for trouble. He went on to explain that if Stalwart employed someone from within the department, then he had to ferret the man out on the quiet. For the department's sake. With the bad press with which the police were already being tarnished, it would look all the worse if word got out that one of the boys in blue had jumped ship for

Stalwart. Therefore, Steve wanted to be absolutely sure of his suspicions. Then he would confront the man and see what he had to say for himself. In the end, Sue had seen his reasoning. To avoid all suspicion, his injury had to be kept secret.

Gil McEwen barrelled into the foyer, trailing a pungent cloud of cigar smoke. His eyes locked on Steve and he moved in.

"By damn, where did you get to?"

The young couple had prepared a cover story.

"I was up sick all night," explained Steve. "Yesterday's feed went down but wouldn't stay down. I was all in by the time I hit the sack. Dead to the world – until Sue came pounding on my door. Sorry, Gil."

As McEwen trusted Steve with his life, he accepted the lie without hesitation – a fact not lost on Steve Thatcher whose gut churned, for real, at having to exploit his friend's faith in him.

"You're here," McEwen concluded. "That's good enough for me. We've got a mountain of work. Still no sign of Metcalf though. Everyone else is on the clock. You know anything about him?"

Steve Thatcher recalled the perfect, right out of the Academy, three-point stance a Stalwart shooter had assumed before hurling a bullet at the Moon Man – the shot that had burned a groove in his shoulder. There was no proof the hooded gunman had been Metcalf, but it was a place to start investigating.

A group of patrolmen were dragging in a gang of pickpockets. The young men struggled with the officers despite the handcuffs on their wrists. McEwen reached out and seized Steve by the elbow of his injured left arm in order to guide the Detective Sergeant and Sue away from the door so the mob could pass. The grip was intended as a friendly gesture but the pressure McEwen's hard fist exerted sent hot daggers racing up Thatcher's arm.

Steve managed to keep his face impassive as a film of sweat broke out across his forehead. His stoicism was not without its price. Inadvertently, Steve squeezed Sue's hand and the bones ground together. The sudden pain made her yelp. Steve, realizing what he was doing, released her hand immediately.

McEwen turned and regarded his daughter following the outburst but Sue didn't miss a beat. She hastily glanced at her wrist watch and yelped again.

"Oh, my, I'm late!" she exclaimed. "I promised to help at the soup kitchen on Crowne. I'll just leave you boys to it."

With that, Sue rose up on tiptoes and kissed Steve's cheek – making sure not to embrace him – and disappeared through the street doors.

"She's good as gold, she is," McEwen observed, pride in every word.

"Better than I deserve," Steve admitted and meant it.

"Don't talk like that! I'll be proud to have you as a son-in-law." Gil's expression resumed its granite-like appearance. "All right, enough of the mushy stuff. We've got places to go."

The two men fell into step, heading out the back to the police parking garage to acquire a unit.

"Sue told me most of it," Thatcher said on the way, "and I read the paper on the way over. How's the old man bearing up?"

"He's spitting nails, for now. We're going to put him in a better mood before the next sunrise."

"How are we going to do that?" Thatcher asked, dreading the answer.

"We're going to capture the Moon Man!"

The next few hours were a flurry of activity the citizens of Great City would talk about for years. Police dragnets were flung far and wide, the hauls substantial. By one o'clock, the holding cells were at capacity. The press was called in to witness the unloading of every con man, petty thief and syndicate tough guy. The message was clear: the GCPD was on the ball and getting the job done.

However this was only half of the story. For every criminal the police took off the street, Stalwart Security added their own collar. They foiled the attempted robbery of the largest branch of the City National Bank. Gil McEwen and Stephen Thatcher broke up a counterfeiting ring while trying to get a line on the Moon Man. The Stalwart unit prevented the kidnapping of Clive Blake, the advertising man. A prostitution ring was raided by officers from the GCPD... And so it went.

Like a pair of prizefighters, the police and Stalwart Security went toe to toe preventing crime and competing for the lion's share of the spotlight. Reporters sacrificed shoe leather bouncing from one big announcement to the next. As the afternoon wore on, there was no end in sight.

For Gil McEwen the triumphs were bittersweet for hours of working informants and hunting leads had provided not one shred of solid information on the Moon Man's whereabouts.

Steve was all in but was both inspired and amazed at the stamina for Gil McEwen. The man, thirty years his senior, still had the burning light of justice in his eyes and his hard hands gripped the wheel like it was a crook's scrawny neck. Steve had managed to mask his injured arm throughout the day although there had been a few close calls.

It was end of shift for Gil and Steve, the deepening twilight held an eerie calm in the wake of all of the police activity as McEwen tooled their unit along the icy streets. Neither of the two policemen had uttered one word about calling it a day.

The radio squawked.

"Listeners, this just in. Stalwart Security has called a press conference at the old Davis Hotel. It's due to start any minute. They claim to have eliminated the Moon Man! Stay tuned for details."

"They're playing our song!" McEwen crowed, shifting in his seat. "By damn that's not far from here! Hang on! Maybe they netted the guy!"

He stomped on the gas and the auto surged forward.

"Gil," Steve began, "it's got to be a publicity stunt. This Moon Man stuff."

"Why do you say that?" Gil demanded. "He's about the only crook we didn't bring in today. Damn him!"

Steve Thatcher could not reveal why he was sure Gil was wrong about the Moon Man's capture.

As the Moon Man last night, Steve had been in the process of robbing a Kane Foods long suspected of charging outrageous prices for goods in a low income neighbourhood hit hard by the Depression. Everything had been proceeding smoothly until Stalwart thugs had unleashed a hail of lead at him.

The Moon Man had evaded capture by commandeering one of their cars outside the store. Murder River had been the pre-arranged meeting place for Angel Dargan and the auto was the Moon Man's ticket away from the gunfire.

Only the thugs had had other cars waiting. The chase was on! The Moon Man had reached the river scant seconds ahead of pursuit and was almost at Suicide Leap when the Stalwart chariot had put on a last spurt and forced him off the road, ultimately driving him into the woods in a hail of Thompson fire.

The Moon Man had been grazed, a hot dagger lancing down one arm. The private army closed in. Thinking fast, Steve had removed the black cloak and distinctive spherical dome and floated them down the river to throw the armed pursuers off the scent, convince them the Moon Man had fallen under their barrage.

And they'd believed it.

Only a few copies of the uniquely designed Argus glass globe had ever been made. This one was Steve's last replacement, and now it was gone forever. The Moon Man had not been hauled in to face justice as Gil McEwen hoped, but, yes, the Stalwart boys had succeeded where the Great City police had failed.

Stalwart Security had brought about the final end of the Moon Man. And the end of Chief Peter Thatcher's stellar career. The venerable old officer would be forever remembered as the man who failed to capture the Moon Man.

Gil voiced his concerns and it was as if the Lieutenant was reading Steve's mind. "It galls me to say it," he said in conclusion, "but I wish the Moon Man was still on the loose. That would give those Stalwart boys a black eye! And we'd still have a chance to save the Chief's reputation!"

Steve could not tell McEwen that Peter Thatcher's fate was sealed. There was no Moon Man anymore.

"Gil," he said at last, "Stalwart is playing games with us. The Moon Man must have realized he can't beat the combined forces of Great City's finest and a private security force. Whoever he is, he must have pulled up stakes and moved on."

"I don't believe that!" McEwen countered. "He's a rat! You've seen that fancy mask of his? You know as well as I do that Argus glass was used by the Speak Easies, during Prohibition, so the customers swilling illegal booze could see a raid approaching and the cops couldn't see in. You get me? The Moon Man doesn't want anyone to see what's underneath that mask because he knows he's rotten to the core. He's a dirty thief who likes to rub our noses in it. No, he stayed put, laughing at us. Well, if that Stalwart crowd has clapped him in irons, that means the Law gets the Moon Man next. If it's the last official thing I do for the Chief, I'm going to personally strap that thieving murderer into the chair myself! The Moon Man will burn!"

Stalwart Security had taken over the vacant Davis Hotel – a once impressive white granite tower of fifteen stories that had fallen into disrepair. Gil swung around to the side lot and had to brake hard. Reporters scurried in every direction, darting between the parked autos.

A long line of cars stretched away from the vertical auto park attached to the side of the building.

The vertical auto park resembled a flattened Ferris wheel 105 feet high and constructed entirely of steel. The apparatus contained twenty-four cradles revolving on endless chains. Motorists wanting to use the system drove on to one of the empty cradles at street level, set their brakes, exited their vehicle, and retrieved a ticket with the cradle number from the automated machine before stepping clear. A metal barrier then swung down and the Ferris wheel-like device revolved, hauling the car up into the air while a fresh, empty cradle swung down for the next auto. Another option was to ride up with one's vehicle to the desired floor, then use the building's fire escape to enter the desired floor.

Reporters anxious for a scoop hoped to do just that and crowded around the soaring lattice of steel. The steady thrum of the seventy-five horsepower engine revolving the wheel and the clank of strong steel was all but drowned out by the shouts and horn honks of the converging vehicles. The harried lift operator stood before the machine yelling at the drivers to use the ground lot. The news vehicles pressed close regardless.

McEwen was having none of that. He nudged the unit into the mass of cars at the front of the line. Fists waved, curses were hurled. McEwen's badge had some effect on quieting the frustrated throng.

The lift operator remained unmoved. Gil raged and threatened but the lift operator held firm that vertical parking was reserved for Stalwart personnel and directed the police car to the ground lot. The Lieutenant growled and twisted the wheel.

Steve Thatcher had to jog to keep up with McEwen as he waded through the throng to the front doors. The lieutenant's broad shoulders moved the people gathered around the entrance while Thatcher tried to protect his injured arm from the pressing mass of humanity.

The lobby wasn't much better. With only a single elevator working in the newly re-opened tower, everyone wanted to go up first lest they miss the start of the press conference. Finally Gil had to threaten the next man who got in their way with jail time for obstructing justice. The throng parted and the two detectives grinned at each other as the operator closed the doors. They had the car to themselves.

The elevator opened on a musty hallway that was a shadow of its former self. The hotel had been closed for more than a decade and the disuse was evident. Paint peeled here and there. A musty odor pervaded. At the end of the hallway was what had at one time been a luxurious banquet room framed by arched, stained-glass windows now barely discernable through a layer of grime. The sad state of the room did not discourage the assembled visitors. Chairs had been arranged in front of a dais and every seat was taken.

Gil and Steve pushed to the front of the stage.

The two cops did not like what they saw.

The hall was ringed by Stalwart personnel – large men dressed in tuxedoes with brown executioner hoods concealing their features. Only their eyes blazed out of holes cut in the loose masks. The men were armed, cradling rifles and shotguns. Hand guns were also in evidence. Gil's first instinct was to haul them all in to check their permits. Steve Thatcher had a different reaction to the armed men. He remembered them from the moonlit chase of the night before. The chase that had brought about the end of the Moon Man.

A hooded speaker stepped up to the microphone. The room fell silent.

"Fellow citizens of Great City," the man's deep voice boomed. "Thank you all for coming. Please do not be alarmed at my appearance. As the police are unable to protect the people of Great City, my colleagues and myself must appear before you masked in this manner for fear of reprisals against us for the good work we have undertaken. The day will come when we will complete the work the police could not accomplish. When that day comes, and it is coming soon, we will be able to walk amongst you unmasked. For the present, you are here on a very special day for this city – one that will be remembered for years to come." He raised his right hand high above his head. In his fist was a blood-spattered black glove. "Do you see this? This is all that remains of the Moon Man!"

A murmur rippled through the crowd. More than one sharp eye turned accusingly to where Gil McEwen and Stephen Thatcher stood to one side.

This reaction by some of the gathered reporters did not escape the speaker. He jabbed a finger at the two officers.

"Now you see the failure of Great City's finest. For months they have wasted taxpayer's hard earned money hunting futilely for the Moon Man! Stalwart Security, in a mere three days dedicated to protecting the honest citizenry, has removed this scourge from our streets. We cornered the thief last night, and, in a hail of gunfire, wiped him out. Stalwart operatives saw his lifeless body in Murder River, being carried out to sea with the rest of the detritus. The Moon Man is dead, ladies and gentlemen. And Great City has Stalwart Security to thank for it! Stalwart Security will keep the streets safe! Such is our promise!"

The room erupted into a cacophony of incredulity and stunned surprise. The speaker held the glove up higher and turned his body so that everyone assembled could see the trophy. Flashbulbs popped like lightning. Reporters pressed around the two officers, their faces grim.

"Too tight," Gil hissed at Steve Thatcher. "Let's get some elbow room."

With derisive gibes ringing in their ears from the speaker, McEwen and Thatcher withdrew through a side door. This gave on another hallway, one with unfinished walls and ceilings, dangling wires brushed the crowns of their hats.

"That mob wants our blood," Steve observed.

"They'll get it, too," McEwen agreed, then his face fell. "If what that mook says is true, then it really is the end for your dad, Steve. The Chief really is finished! They'll run him out on a rail and me along with him. We failed him, son. We failed him!"

The anguish Steve felt at being the cause of his father's downfall was beyond words. It was a wound he'd bear the rest of his days for he was powerless to do anything about it.

There were more pressing worries at the moment. The doors behind them bulged with the crowd of reporters pushing against it.

"We've got to get out of here," Steve said. He glanced at the nearby stairwell but the sound of pounding feet rushing up nixed that idea.

They started down the corridor. Immediately shouts reached them. The doors to the banquet room held. These shouts came from armed, hooded men stepping out of the stair well behind them.

"Stop! What do you two thing you're doing?" the voices yelled. "You can't go that way!"

The fire escape was directly ahead and it was the police officers' intention to use it to get out onto the vertical auto park and ride it down to the lot, bypassing the reporters swarming all over the building.

The two men ignored the shouts behind them and continued on.

A pair of shotguns cocked loudly in the quiet hallway behind them. "Stop! We won't say it again."

"Get that window open," McEwen hissed at Steve, meaning the exit to the fire escape. He whirled on the armed men and stalked brazenly towards the lowered muzzles of the shotguns. "Who the hell do you think you're talking to? By damn, you point your weapons at police officers? I'll lock you all up and throw away the key!"

Oddly McEwen's action seemed to calm the men. They placed their guns across their shoulders and muffled laughter echoed from beneath their hoods.

"Relax fellas, it's only McEwen," one of the men said. "You're through in this town. We've got things under control now. Why don't you run along and leave us to clean up your mess?"

This open dismissal galled McEwen but he wasn't about to let them see it. He demanded to see the permits for the weapons. The men shrugged offhandedly and dug for their wallets while McEwen kept up a righteous tirade to keep the hooded men distracted.

Meanwhile Steve was at the window. He turned the latch. A set of double doors to his right were not tightly closed and he saw evidence of movement between them. Low voices. Scraping as if heavy objects were being moved. He leaned his head to one side. He could not distinctly hear what they were saying but thought he recognized one of the voices.

It sounded like the voice of Detective Bob Metcalf.

The two Stalwart guards had returned their gun permits to their wallets and had taken notice of Steve at the end of the hall.

"Get away from there!" they bellowed past McEwen who turned to face Steve Thatcher.

"We're riding down that way," McEwen explained. He whirled his gat into his hand and let it dangle at his side. "Try to stop us. Ready, Steve?"

"All set!" Steve called back over his shoulder. As he did so, Metcalf's voice grew louder for a moment. The man must have moved past the closed doors.

"Get the stuff stowed!" Metcalf was saying to unseen others in the shut up room. "There'll be more when the crowd clears. Then – "

The speaker moved away from the door, the voice faded.

Steve thrust open the window and put one foot on the fire escape. McEwen was right beside him, having backed down the corridor in order to keep the armed thugs in sight.

The guards remained frozen in place as if any sudden movement would bring disaster. McEwen's lips twisted at them, then he returned his gun to its holster and stepped out to join Steve on the fire escape, closing the window behind him.

Before they stepped onto the platform of the vertical park tower, Steve tried to peer into the window of the room from which the voices had issued. The window was coated in grime. He could not see in.

McEwen whistled shrilly down at the car lift operator after they had stepped onto the platform and were standing next to a roadster more than one hundred feet above the street. The operator glanced up and McEwen's

"McEwen whistled ...down at the...operator..."

gold shield was unmistakeable. He jabbed down with one thick finger. The operator got the message and worked the controls.

The tone was sombre on the ride back to the station. Gil McEwen berated himself silently for his failure to capture the Moon Man – failure which had ruined the reputation of the one man he respected and admired above all others. Every few seconds, he pounded the steering wheel in frustration while his eyes blazed out across the icy road ahead.

Steve Thatcher's heart was leaden. The Moon Man had ruined the life's work of his father. And yet, it was only the Moon Man who could redeem the man. He recalled what Gil had said earlier. If the Moon Man could reappear, it would counter the claims the leader of Stalwart Security had made. If the Moon Man was still alive, it would sully the credibility of the masked force.

It was all so much smoke. The robe and glass dome were gone, swept out to sea.

But nothing had cooled the ardour of Steve Thatcher's dedication. He had become the Moon Man to serve a higher law than the law of man. Every penny of the money he stole from thieves was crucial in saving the lives of others suffering terribly during the economic catastrophe. People were hungry, sick, hopeless and lost. The Moon Man, through Angel Dargan, had been their helping hand, their chance at a fresh start. Well, if the Moon Man was finished, then he would continue the fight in another guise. He may be powerless to undo the harm to his father's reputation or save Gil McEwen's job, but, hell, he could still do some good in the world.

Steve Thatcher settled back in his seat and glared out at the black road ahead. The way before him did not seem quite so dark as it had a moment before.

Later that night, a sedan glided silently by the rear of police headquarters. Across the bleak alley, there stood a dark, disreputable-looking garage. A faded, sagging sign nailed on the door read: To Let.

The sedan swung slowly from the street and idled before the doors. The automobile's headlamps beamed upon the door and blinked – three times quickly, then twice. A discreetly placed, sensitive photo-electric cell caught the signal. On well-oiled hinges, the garage doors, tugged by hidden mechanisms, slid open. The sedan eased into the black maw. The doors glided quietly shut behind the vehicle.

A figure obscured by gloom, stepped from the car and moved to a small office partitioned off in the corner. The figure froze. The office was occupied. The dim yellow glow of an old bulb threw the distorted shadow of a figure on the office wall.

The shape outside the office drew a .45 from a jacket pocket. The shadow on the office wall contorted as the unknown figure within moved about.

The door creaked open. The spectre outside raised the automatic.

"Boss," a familiar voice whispered. "Is that you?"

The figure outside visibly relaxed. The .45 drooped.

"Angel?"

"Boss!" Angel Dargan threw the door open. "Thank God you're all right!"

Steve Thatcher took a half step into the cone of light spilling from the open office door. On his face, sorrow was etched. He had come to tell Dargan that the Moon Man was finished.

Dargan raised both horny hands up in a placating gesture. "Hang on, Boss."

Dargan retreated into the dim office and returned holding a familiar black case the size of an overnight bag in one hand. In his other large fist, he clutched the black robe of the Moon Man. He set the case down across the sill and lay the robe reverently on top.

"The glass was dry but I didn't put the robe inside," he explained. "It was still wet after I cleaned it."

Perplexed, Thatcher reached out for the case, drew it into the shadows with him. Dargan watched it disappear into the darkness. The latches snapped and an exclamation that was half-gasp, half-sob sounded in the stygian expanse.

There was the rustle of black cloth across strong shoulders. Fingers trembling with adrenalin squeaked across mirrored Argus glass. The excited breathing was suddenly muffled slightly and there was an audible click as the two halves of glass snapped shut. Moonlight from the high window on one wall etched the sphere which appeared to be floating above the floor of the garage. The globe moved forward.

Dargan stepped back into the office.

The Moon Man crossed the threshold!

"Nice to have you back, Boss."

The Moon Man was suddenly overcome as the full implication of Dargan's actions hit him. The glass-domed head dipped. Then it straightened and faced the ex-pugilist. The Moon Man put a hand on Dargan's shoulder and squeezed. "God bless you, Angel!"

The praise brought a gleam to Dargan's eyes which quelled any response the tough boxer was about to make. Instead he glanced down at the bare hand on his shoulder and said, "You're going to need some new gloves, Boss."

The Moon Man chuckled warmly. He gave Dargan's shoulder one last squeeze and released it.

From the pocket of his worn coat, Dargan withdrew a set of black leather gloves. "Here. Call 'em a late Christmas present."

The Moon Man drew the gloves tight around his hands and the transformation was complete.

The two men got down to business. The Moon Man asked for a report on the current distribution of money he had stolen to help the needy. With the previous night's haul lost, the funds were desperately low and there were still so many people in need of help. The Moon Man's resolve hardened as Dargan told him about the orphanage needing penicillin, tenement families left destitute in the wake of a suspicious fire that had destroyed the building and all of their worldly goods. There was the widow whose husband, an ice man, had been caught in a gun battle between two gangs. The staff of a hairbrush company left out in the cold when the owner closed up the plant and fled the country with the capital. Racketeers squeezing store owners. And so it went.

The message was clear: It was imperative that the Moon Man strike. With the combined forces of the police and Stalwart Security poised to stop him, the dangers were never greater. But there was no choice, really. Too many lives depended on the aid that only the Moon Man could render.

But maybe the Moon Man could help even the odds.

"Angel, I'm going to look into Stalwart Security. I have my suspicions they are up to something illicit. If I can turn up facts, something that will run them out of town, then we'll have an easier time getting the funds we need to help those you mentioned."

"Easier time!" Dargan barked. "You've got the entire police force after you. Boss, I don't like it. If anything should happen to you – "

"Rest easy, Angel. They haven't caught me yet."

"Okay, Boss. You know best. Just be careful!"

"Always," the Moon Man replied and vanished into the night.

The night was bitterly cold but the fire of a new beginning warmed the Moon Man as he drove along the deserted street. The power to help Peter

Thatcher had been restored – power the Moon Man had been certain was lost forever. It was a second chance he would not squander.

The Moon Man parked the roadster on a quiet side street three blocks from the headquarters of Stalwart Security. He was on a residential street, the house fronts dark and silent. The snow had begun to fall late in the day but was already piled high on the lawns. Snowmen, abandoned unfinished at nightfall, were left headless and trunk-less on every other lawn.

His destination was the home of Bob Metcalf. It lay dead ahead. The Moon Man sidled across the snowy lawns toward it.

The approaching roar of an auto engine made him freeze. He whirled. A squad car was trundling up the street on routine patrol. The wide beams of the headlamps illuminated the house fronts. The Moon Man was out in the open, trapped. It would be impossible for the glow of the lamps not to find him.

Thinking fast, he took the only option open to him.

Darting to one of the unfinished snowmen, the Moon Man crouched behind it and rested the mirrored glass globe atop the headless creation. The Moon Man's eyes tracked the approach of the squad car through the mirrored surface which, he hoped, would appear as the glistening head of the snowman concealing him.

Seconds dragged as the car drew near. The Moon Man held his breath, every muscle tight for flight. Then the squad car ambled by with no hitch in its progress. The ruse had worked.

The home of Bob Metcalf was the next house over. Metcalf had two young boys. The sled and toy shovels sticking out of the snow of the front yard were obstacles the Moon Man angled around. The front of the house was a black silent face. Light spilled from a side window across a narrow path to light the wall of the house next door. The Moon Man made for it.

A parlor window. Seated within, on a rocker by the fire, was Metcalf's wife. The hour being late, the boys were sleeping. There was no sign of the man of the house.

The Moon Man was about to abandon the spot when a phone rang inside. The mirrored sphere at the window jerked. The phone rang again, dully, muffled.

Evelyn Metcalf rose from her seat and hurried to the jangling instrument. It lay on a hall table just outside the parlor door. She picked up the receiver.

The Moon Man strained his ears but could not make out the words. The window was closed tight, locked against the wintry night.

Evelyn Metcalf was speaking into the receiver. It was imperative the Moon Man hear what the woman said.

Inspiration struck him.

Gently so as to make no sound, the Moon Man pressed the glass bowl against the cold window pane.

Mrs. Metcalf's voice was instantly audible as the vibrations were amplified by the touching glass surfaces.

"Where are you, Bob?" the women asked, worry in her tone. "The boys missed you at supper. I'm worried sick." There was a pause as she listened. "No, I don't understand. Why are you doing this? We need you here! The chance you're taking – "

The Moon Man judged by the woman's actions that the line had gone dead. He stepped away from the window as the woman resumed her seat, tears glistening in her blue eyes.

The evidence against Bob Metcalf was hardly damning, however it didn't look good. More information was essential. As so many were during these hard times, Evelyn Metcalf was left alone in her sorrow.

The Moon Man reached the hotel headquarters of Stalwart Security. Activity there made him cautious in his approach. Men in tuxedos and women in a rainbow array of evening gowns moved in and out of the building in steady streams. The couples smoked, talked, laughed freely, briefly taking the frigid night air to escape the close conditions inside.

Although the Moon Man planned to make his presence known to the people of Great City, this was not the time for exposure. Using the shadows, he crept around to the side of the building where the vertical auto park lanced up at the black sky.

Here another form of activity was taking place. One that drew the interest of the Moon Man. As before a steady stream of automobiles cued up to use the elevator except, this time, the operator directed the sedans into the Ferris wheel device with regularity. In itself, this was not out of the ordinary. Stalwart Security appeared to be hosting a soiree in celebration of their supposed disposal of the Moon Man and as a way to ingratiate themselves deeper amongst the upper crust of society. Granting the rich and powerful of the city access to exclusive parking was a means to that end.

The longer the Moon Man observed the elevator, the more sinister the scene became and the more he began to doubt this conclusion.

For the autos went up, disappearing into the veil of night high above the glow of the streetlamps, their drivers still at the wheel, only to return to the street minutes later and drive off. As a means of timing the procedure, the Moon Man singled out a particular machine as it swung up into the air, then returned to earth, gunned its engine and pulled out of the lot. The auto occupied its cradle for no more than five minutes.

The Moon Man needed to discover what was behind this strange action.

The bitter cold worked to his advantage. The operator used every free moment to return to the little shed on one side of the lot. This narrow dwelling contained a space heater the Moon Man observed him warming himself at before reluctantly exiting to guide the next car into place. For some of the drivers, old hands at the tower's operation the Moon Man guessed, the operator did not come out at all but, rather, huddled with his back to the apparatus as the drivers operated it themselves.

The keen eyes of the Moon Man studied the operation through the impassive, one-way glass of his domed helmet. The cars would come in; the drivers would leave the engines idling as they hurriedly stepped out of the vehicle, reached out of the bay to turn the control handle at the master control, then slammed the barrier down across the rear of their vehicles before dashing back to the warmth of their autos. This took scant seconds but left a span of heartbeats between the time the drivers were back in their cars and the chains clanked taut to lift the machines – seconds during which the Moon Man could approach the machine unseen.

The operator came out, grumbling and shuffling his cold feet along the icy cement. The Moon Man held back as the next car was seen to. One glance at the next in line told the operator that this driver knew the drill and the man jogged gratefully back to his shelter as the car he'd just help position rose into the sky.

The Moon Man inched as close as he dared. The snowfall had intensified to blizzard strength, further obscuring his approach.

The driver of the next car awaited a clear cradle and gunned his machine onto it.

Tensing, the Moon Man prepared to leap.

The driver, a rake-thin scrawny type hopped out and slapped at the control feverishly, chattering curses to the cold as he worked. So chilled was the man that he did not even bother to lower the barrier. Instead he darted back to the warmth of the car.

The Moon Man made his move. Whisper quiet, he slunk onto the cradle, crouching so as not to be seen through the rear-view mirror by the driver. Like a ball player sliding home, he eased underneath the automobile, angling the glass globe atop his shoulders to ensure the operator remained oblivious.

The cradle was yanked by the chains and began its journey upwards.

It was a tight fit under the rear of the vehicle for the fragile glass of the Moon Man's globular mask. Choking exhaust would have overcome him if not for the protective sphere and the oxygen trapped within.

The cradle jolted to a halt. The plume of exhaust cut off. Worn, salt-stained shoes scrapped across the cradle as the driver stepped out. Stepping quickly around to the trunk, the driver opened the lid and bent over the container. From his position under the vehicle, the Moon Man could see the crease in the man's cheap trousers.

Grunting, legs braced, the spindly man struggled with something heavy inside the trunk. It clanged down on the rear fender.

"Easy with that," A voice cautioned from within the hotel. The glass panel entry was open. "You trying to wake the dead?"

"How about giving me a hand instead of flapping your gums?" the driver insisted.

"Not my job, pal."

The driver hurled epithets at the man, but proceeded to tumble the heavy steamer trunk to the floor of the cradle and slide it to the fire escape window.

The guard watched the man's struggle. The grating noise seemed to get louder as it echoed off the wall.

"Keep it down, will ya?" the guard warned. "Hang on! I'll help with the blasted thing!"

Feet scraped, grunts sounded, then all was quiet at the window.

Cautiously, the Moon Man emerged from his hiding place. It was almost pitch-black this high up. Glancing down he saw the lit streets ghostly and silent a hundred feet below. Seconds were fleeting.

Using the car as cover, the Moon Man approached the wall of the building. The guard had accompanied the driver into the room with the double doors. The window had been left open and was unattended. Voices reached the Moon Man. There was also the sound of low moaning and sobbing.

"Two more hauls tonight, boys," it was Metcalf who was speaking! "Put the cash and bonds in the safe. Use the steamer for the jewelry. There're enough barrels for the furs. Step lively, now. We're not getting any younger and fleecing Great City's big wigs takes a lot out of a guy!"

Thoughts churned through the mind of the Moon Man. Stalwart Security was running an extortion racket. Autos loaded with stolen goods drove in, then using the dark cover of the vertical auto park; the thieves unloaded the stuff right above the heads of the police. His eyes grew grim at the thought of Metcalf, a police officer, involved in this illegal activity.

"Benny! Shut those two up, will you?" A loud shout reached the Moon Man through the glass. "We can't hear ourselves think!" The harsh rasp of footsteps could be heard. "If you'd come across right off like the rest of them you'd have no worries, friend."

A loud thud resounded from behind the doors. A woman screamed.

The Moon Man eased the window open and hopped down to the bare floor, landing as softly as a cat. The corridor was dim. No other guards were about. Nudging the door open a fraction of an inch, The Moon Man peered into the room. Including the driver and the guard who had vacated his post, he counted five hooded, armed men in the room. The Moon Man withdrew a shiny automatic from a slit in the folds of his black robe. He did not hesitate.

Rearing back, the Moon Man kicked the doors open, stood framed in the entrance. "Nobody move!"

The room was the mirror image of the banquet hall at the opposite end of the corridor. However this one was a sagging, mouldering disused affair. Figures were dimly visible in the faint light of oil lamps here and there. He detected two bound captives along one wall of the spacious room where a makeshift laboratory was arranged along a long, narrow table. Wide eyes goggled at the spectre before them.

"The Moon Man!" roared Metcalf. "Blast him!"

Trunks and barrels crashed to the ground as desperate hands pawed at sidearms.

The Moon Man ducked behind a low stack of trunks. His injured shoulder throbbed with the impact. Bullets thudded into the leather and steel. Swinging low, the Moon Man brought his gun to bear. Flames stabbed and lead drove into the chest of the skinny driver who groaned and fell, knocking over the oil lamp at his feet, spreading flame.

From the corner of one eye, the Moon Man saw a well-dressed couple bound to wooden chairs. The man, some silver at his temples, looked distinguished. The woman, younger, his wife. Strange convulsions racked the man's body while his wife could only gape in mute horror.

Return fire drove the Moon Man from cover. He fired two shots, heard one gasp and the clear tinkle of breaking glass.

A Thompson opened up. Metcalf's finger was on the trigger.

Chunks of the wall were ripped out scant inches behind the Moon Man as he ran for a stack of crates. The Moon Man returned fire before diving for cover with thoughts of reloading. Feet scraped as men scattered. Someone knocked over another of the oil lamps in their haste and a sheet of flame fanned out across the dry wooden floor.

The Moon Man moved to draw closer to the bound captives. Metcalf tried to block the play with the Thompson and the vials and test tubes on the lab table jumped and shattered. Stray shots found the bound man and his queer convulsions ceased amidst spurts of crimson. The woman screamed.

The spreading flames convinced one man to give up the fight. He bolted for the door just as Metcalf let loose and was cut down in the storm of lead.

The Moon Man risked a shot at Metcalf. It went wide but the crooked cop sought cover.

The Moon Man slapped a fresh clip into his weapon as he lunged for the chair restraining the woman. He dragged it to safety behind the pile of crates. It was a temporary reprieve. The room was alight now, flames licking up the walls. The only exit was at the Moon Man's back. The path to it was in Metcalf's field of fire.

Using a pocket knife, the Moon Man slashed the thick cord of the terrified woman's bonds.

"My h-husband," she sobbed, her glassy-eyed stare seemed transfixed by the flames. "Force h-him to p-pay... h-he refused! T-They injected h-him w-with something... "

"There's no time for that now," the Moon Man hissed. He detected movement from behind. Whirling and firing, he put a bullet through the hood of the man creeping up from behind. This action brought a staccato reply from the Thompson. "I will keep our opponent pinned down. On my signal break for the door and get out of the building. It's tinder-dry, the whole place is going to go up. Take the stairs. Do not use the elevator."

The Moon Man peered around the corner. Thick smoke roiled around the place.

"Go!" he hissed to the woman as he stood up and expended an entire clip at Metcalf.

The woman, stunned, shakily regained her feet. She moved, dazed, uncertain.

The Moon Man saw Metcalf break cover, the Thompson swinging up.

The room was alight now, flames licking up the walls.

The automatic barked. Hot lead sought the man but missed by inches. The Thompson chattered, shots roared for a heartbeat, then the weapon jammed.

The sound caught the woman's addled ears and she took a step in the direction of the sound.

"Not that way!" the Moon Man bellowed.

The windows shattered from the heat. Cold air rushed in to fan the wall of flames. In seconds the room was ablaze, the ceiling gave way. This distracting sound was all the Moon Man needed. He darted around the box of crates and came right at Metcalf.

But the corrupt officer had guessed this move. With animal cunning he pounced upon the woman. One arm clamped around her throat, the other seized a syringe from the burning lab table.

The Moon Man, framed by the sole exit behind him stood ghostly in the red-tinged glow of the room. He raised his automatic, the bore pointed at Metcalf's head. "Don't!"

"Drop the gat!" Metcalf spat. "I've seen what this stuff can do. One prick and she'll be dead before she hits the floor!"

Of that the Moon Man had no doubt. The woman had said her husband had been injected and the man's last minutes seemed tortured before lead had mercifully cut them short.

The flames lanced through the ceiling. Cold air fed the blaze and the flames danced roaring along the roof. Thick smoke made breathing difficult although the Moon Man, encased in his spherical mask had a slight oxygen supply.

Muffled cries sounded everywhere as the fire rushed to engulf all. Feet pounded, doors slammed, glass shattered. The party-goers in the room at the end of the opposite end of the hall broke in wild panic, cramming into the elevator, overloading the car, their panic making them oblivious to the fact that it was not in operation. The cables snapped and the car plunged to the ground, killing all aboard.

Amidst this pandemonium, the Moon Man and Metcalf faced each other as the fire raged. The hooded officer's eyes were frantic, desperate. They darted from the flames to the impassive globe of the Moon Man's face as seconds hurtled by.

"I'll kill her!" he warned.

The Moon Man could not risk a shot in the smoke. He eased closer. Knowing the mirrored sphere of his helmet reflected Metcalf and the woman, he took another half-step closer.

"Look, Metcalf!" he said. "Observe your hand clutching at the woman's throat, the terror in her eyes. See the needle in your fist. You were a police officer. Is this who you wish to be now?"

The Moon Man took another step closer. Metcalf could see himself reflected in the mirrored glass. It was one reason why the Moon Man had selected the Argus glass helmet at the start of his crusade – in order that the unjust, the corrupt could see themselves at their lowest moment, the instant of their downfall and remember.

"You have a wife and family," the Moon Man intoned. "Would you have them see you like this? A criminal!"

Metcalf's eyes wavered. The syringe lowered until it was at the woman's midsection. "H-How do you know who I am? How do you know?"

"Release the woman!" the Moon Man barked.

"No! There's no going back!" Metcalf spat. "I had no choice! Don't you understand? Bills to pay, mouths to feed. A cop's salary... it just isn't enough!"

A portion of the ceiling crashed down behind him, drowning out whatever he was about to say. Metcalf jumped, his grip loosened on the woman. The Moon Man leaped in and pistol-whipped the hooded head.

The Moon Man placed a gloved hand in the center of the woman's back and shoved her towards the flame framed door. She disappeared through the exit.

Metcalf moaned where he sprawled. Police sirens wailed through the lusty surge of flames. He shook his head and came up in a crouch.

"I'm not going over! Never!"

Metcalf sprang to his feet. Driven by wild panic he bolted for the exit. A group of hooded crooks were at the open elevator doors, guns dangling, unsure of their next move as they stared down at the grisly sight below. He roughly shoved into them.

"Got to get away! The Moon Man! Got to!"

They sought to restrain him, but he tore free and dove through the open elevator doors. Too late he realized that only a dark, rushing descent to death awaited him. His screams echoed down the vacant shaft before being cut short.

The rattled group has allowed the woman to take the stairs and considered this means of escape. Fear held them from flight. It was not the fire that scared them.

The Moon Man appeared at the end of the corridor and the group was spurred into action.

"There he is! Get him before he reaches the fire escape!"

The Moon Man moved like lightning. The paneled window had shattered allowing for an easy exit on to the fire escape now covered with snow. The vertical auto park lay a step beyond.

Seconds ahead of the men rushing up the corridor, the Moon Man slid along the wet metal landing and hopped onto a cradle. A sedan parked on it provided much needed cover as guns exploded behind him. Bullets spanged and winged off the steel structure. Windshield glass shattered and the auto rocked from multiple impacts.

Bending low, the Moon Man returned fire from underneath the machine.

Thinking fast, he tore off a long strip of the cloak he wore. Wadding it up, he crept to the gas tank, opened the chamber and wadded the material in.

Return fire drove him back to safety at the trunk of the car. Quick shots from the automatic drove the men back. They had no desire to expose themselves on the fire escape and the shattered window was too narrow for all of them to safely bring their weapons to bear.

The Moon Man lit the wad wedged into the tank. The explosion would remove the threat from the window. Of course it would remove him as well if he did not distance himself from the makeshift bomb.

However fate was about to play a hand.

The auto park operator, detecting the ruckus high above his head, mistook it for the sounds of his fellow Stalwart elements in trouble and started the revolving system. The Moon Man and the automobile about to explode began descending to street level.

As the operator had a group of armed Stalwart men around him, this spelled doom for the Moon Man. If he stayed put, the explosion would consume him. Leaping to safety would result in his being cut in two by a hail of gun fire.

There was only one option left to him and he took it.

Leaping up, the Moon Man seized the edge of the cradle above him and pulled himself up. The wound in his shoulder was like a hot coal under the inflamed skin. The space between the edge of the cradle and the brick wall was narrow and the mirrored sphere just managed it.

He repeated this action in the hopes that two steel-plate floors would be sufficient to deflect the coming blast.

The elevator continued down as the flame crawled up the cloth wedged into the gas tank.

Stalwart mob members saw the streetlight glint off the Moon Man's gleaming mask. Guns began firing from below. The men above added their fire to the mix and soon the entire steel elevator was a firework of sparking bullet hits.

At last the cradle with the bomb aboard reached the ground, the operator shut down the machine. The gunmen piled in, expecting to find the Moon Man. One of them noticed the gas tank with the tongue of flame now crawling inside and bellowed.

They beat a hasty retreat. One of them shoved the operator aside and threw the lever to take the bomb car heavenward. The chains clanked and the cradle reversed direction.

Too late.

The gas tank exploded. A sheet of flame and smoke roared out of the narrow steel confines, engulfing the operator and the firing men. Howls of agony sounded as the men not killed instantly by the blast were burned alive.

The blast shook the structure. The Moon Man gripped a stanchion.

With the operator and the ground forces dead, there was no one to stop the mechanism. The Moon Man was slowly rising upwards to the waiting guns of the men still in the burning building.

Checking the load of his automatic, eyes grim behind the mirrored glass, the Moon Man made his ascent.

The men above howled their triumph and let loose with a flurry of pot shots. Hot lead mingled with the icy flakes driving down. The shots struck well wide of the Moon Man.

That was about to change, however, as the elevator was carrying the Moon Man back up to the waiting guns. Perhaps he could buy some time.

Gripping his automatic by the barrel, he smashed the driver side window of the car he shared the cradle with. Thrusting an arm inside, he released the hand brake. Using every ounce of strength he rolled the machine forward until the front bumper scraped along the brick wall, eschewing sparks. The Moon Man reset the brake.

This slowed the ascent of the elevator but did not halt it entirely. That happened when the bumper impacted a jutting, stone window sill. Steel met cement and the elevator mechanism jammed, whining its protest.

On the street, things were happening. Approaching police had pulled up just as the explosion erupted. The blast had rocked the building and shattered a telephone pole. Electric wires snaked across the street in the direction of the crowd that had gathered. Gil McEwen, in the lead car, tore his gaze from the burning building and resigned himself to getting the onlookers to safety. It looked as if the building would go any minute.

A fact not lost on the Moon Man. He had obtained temporary reprieve from the Stalwart mob but his position was not ideal. With a stomach-dropping judder, the bumper of the car cracked the concrete sill. The battle between the two would soon be decided. Another jerk and the structure rattled.

This was the least of the Moon Man's worries. Stray bullets fired at him from above and below had punctured the gas tanks of the other automobiles on the cradles. Pungent gas fumes wormed beneath the domed mask. The auto park was bathed in gasoline. Once the bumper either cleared the sill or sheared off, the elevator would resume its ascent and the Stalwart gang would resume firing. One spark and the gasoline would ignite. Meanwhile gas dripped inexorably down towards the fire raging at the base of the structure.

Daring all, the Moon Man began crawling through the guts of the machinery to the cradles at the opposite side. He was on the side going upwards. If he could make it across the machine would carry him down, away from harm when it resumed motion. While the fire was keeping the police busy, he might make his escape.

It was a heart-stopping climb through the steel lattice-work. With the thick steel beams poised like bobbing guillotine-blades above and below him, held back only by the car bumper which could snap clear at any second, the Moon Man risked being sliced in two.

His heels rang on the opposite cradle. He yanked the robe clear of the steel framework a split second before the bumper clanged free and the elevator resumed operation. The cradle which held the Moon Man proceeded downwards.

However this was hardly time to celebrate. The men above would open fire any second.

Taking a chance, The Moon Man tried the door of the roadster on the cradle next to him. It was unlocked. He piled inside.

The keys were in the ignition. He ground the starter.

The men above opened fire. A fireball erupted in front of them as the gasoline ignited. Fire raced tracing burning fingers along every inch of the structure. Soon it would find the other gas tanks.

The motor caught. The Moon Man threw the machine into reverse. He could not tell how high up he was but the only other alternative was to be cooked alive.

He stomped on the gas.

Tires squealed on the wet metal. The auto reared out of the elevator just as flame bathed the cradle and the gas tanks of the other cars began to explode in succession.

The Moon Man felt the structure dip as it was torn loose from the wall housing, then the roadster was in mid-air, falling backwards.

Its rear struck the slick concrete of the parking lot a moment later. The Moon Man had been no more than ten feet off the ground when he'd thrown the vehicle into gear. Sparks flew from the rear bumper and the Moon Man rode the auto like a bucking bronco, his grip feverish on the wheel.

All four tires on the ground, the Moon Man pointed the vehicle out of the lot. Behind him the entire elevator parking structure collapsed in a rush of flames and twisting steel.

The Moon Man careened into the street. McEwen, in his efforts to protect the people, had unknowingly cleared the avenue for the Moon Man's escape.

The car tore off up the street. McEwen bellowed his frustration as he ordered squad cars to follow. Two units gave chase, but hulking fire engines swung around the corner seconds after the fleeing auto had cleared the intersection, blocking pursuit. The Moon Man was soon lost in the raging blizzard.

Driving snow obscured the approach the roadster made to the rundown garage. Headlamps flashed the rhythmic sign and the signal penetrated the swirling flakes. The doors parted and the roadster sluiced inside.

Dargan was waiting as the Moon Man stepped out of the auto.

"Thank God you made it back safe and sound, Boss," he said, relief evident in every word. "It's all over the radio. The shoot out. Fire. Explosions. Sheesh, the chances you take!"

"Stalwart Security will not recover from this setback," the Moon Man observed, ignoring Dargan's concern for his safety. He removed the glass sphere. "The city is once again in the right hands."

"If you say so, Boss. But it's going to be rough sledding from here on out."

Stephen Thatcher had saved his father's reputation and preserved his best friend's self-respect. That was all that mattered to him in the end. Also, with the city again under the sole, watchful eye of the police, the

Moon Man could operate once more, bringing much needed money to those in dire straits.

As to that, Dargan's report earlier had not fallen on deaf ears. The road ahead would be hazardous though. The police still had much to prove to the people of Great City. Well, the Moon Man would take the risk. Every penny he put in the hands of the poor kept hope alive.

"What should we do with this machine?" Dargan asked, surveying the wreck. "It's shot full of holes and leaking oil."

"Sell it for scrap," the Moon Man replied, distracted. The few dollars it garnered would be a start on his holy crusade. "Make sure there are no weapons in it. We can't afford too many questions."

"Will do, Boss."

Dargan began inspecting the auto while the Moon Man stepped into the small office to plan strategy for the crimes ahead. With the police gunning for him it really was unwise at present to continue stealing from the rich and corrupt. The needs of Great City's destitute were never ending though. There was no choice in the end. No choice! He would take the risk even if it meant his life.

"Boss, uh, you better come take a look at this."

The Moon Man's spherical head turned at this distraction. He rejoined Dargan.

"What is it, Angel?"

Dargan indicated a large steamer trunk he had hoisted out of the rear of the roadster. The container was four feet wide and three high.

The Moon Man glanced at it as he quickly explained to Dargan the manner in which the Stalwart gang were transporting extorted items.

Dargan fixed the Moon Man with his gaze. "Boss, open it."

The Moon Man stooped. Gloved hands seized the broken latches.

An audible gasp sounded from within the globe mask of the Moon Man as the lid swung open.

Inside, packed tightly, were stacks of one hundred dollar bills. Thousands of them.

A pleased smile stretched the lips beneath the Argus glass. The Moon Man gripped Dargan's shoulder as they stared down at the fortune before them.

Yes, it looked like the Moon Man was free to go into eclipse. For awhile.

Bright sunlight bathed Great City blanketed in a deep coating of fresh snow. Warm rays lanced through the window of Chief Peter Thatcher's office where Gil, Steve and Sue were welcoming the venerable law officer back to work.

The atmosphere was calm this morning as they discussed the sudden disappearance of Stalwart Security.

Gil McEwen was filling them in on the preliminary findings at the burned out building. "The boys poked through the place this morning, found burned up furs, heaps of metal slag that was once jewellery and heaps of ash in a couple of safes. It looked like a giant storeroom for every crook in this city. It was extortion all right. The rich folks surrounded themselves with armed men, men they didn't know. Pretty slick of the Stalwart gang to use crooks in masks to force their clients to pay through the nose for protection. Or else. Those who refused to pay got injected with concentrated snake venom."

Steve Thatcher recalled the convulsions of the dying man prior to the shoot out. Now that Gil had mentioned it, the symptoms added up. "Have any of their clients come clean?"

Gil replied. "No they're not talking! We got most of it from when we rounded up what was left of the gang as they spilled out of the blazing building. The stuff went up to the top floor on that auto park for sorting while the drivers waited, then shares of the loot were packed and driven around to drops for safe keeping."

"How did the round up go?" Chief Thatcher wanted to know.

"Shots fired, but no serious injuries. The drops were isolated, out by the river mostly. Nowhere for the rats to run once we got the drop on them. Hauled them in by the bushel. If only the Moon Man was there! We would have bagged him, too! I bet he was behind the whole thing!"

"Come on, Gil, they held a press conference to announce they got him," Steve reminded them. "And all they had to show for it was a glove. Surely, if the Moon Man was running that show, they'd have furnished more convincing evidence of his death to cover this fact." Thatcher perched jauntily on the corner of his father's desk. "Can't say I blame the rich folks for keeping quiet though. The upper crust has got egg on its collective face – seeing as they would have to come to us, the police, to get justice. They rode the force pretty hard, tried to convince everyone we couldn't do our jobs. Those Stalwart boys being crooks, the high society of Great City look mighty foolish about now."

"That could be, son," Peter Thatcher observed, his kind eyes were thoughtful. "What we do know for certain is that we've seen the last of Stalwart Security. Those that survived the fire are in custody. Good riddance, I say. This is a time where law and order are more important than ever and it pains me that extortionists could come in here and win over the people so quickly. We're going to have to be better at keeping the peace."

"There are a lot of desperate people these days," Sue said, worry crinkling her smooth forehead as she took Steve's hand and gazed up at him. "They need something they can depend on."

"That something is going to be Great City's police force."

"You said it, Chief," Gil said, nodding enthusiastically. "I'll prove that to the Moon Man personally. If I could just get my hands on him… "

THE END

BAD MOON RISING

*T*he Moon Man is my favorite pulp hero.

There, I've said it.

To reach this lofty height he had to dethrone none other than Doc Savage! No easy feat – as many of Doc's villains have learned over the years.

I know what you're thinking and here's the answer to that question you're dying to ask: "Yes, the Moon Man is that good."

The original tales I've torn through (I haven't read all 38... yet) are simply some of the most fun, action-packed, emotionally charged pulp tales I've had the privilege to read. And that includes Classic Pulp, New Pulp and everything in-between. Learning that the Moon Man was public domain, for me, was like learning that the copyrights on Doc Savage and the Shadow had expired! Are you kidding me? I can write all the Moon Man tales I want? Yup, count me in.

The anthology you've got in your hands and, I hope, are enjoying was long planned by Airship 27 though it seemed to be taking forever to come together – hey, it happens sometimes. Then suddenly, boom, the ol' Airship had the book on the launch pad, ready and waiting for my contribution. This took me by surprise but I hit the ground running.

First, I snagged the first 19 original tales by Frederick C. Davis courtesy of a great hardcover collection from the mid-80s and dove in. Wow! I read them one after the other and each was so good I immediately wanted to read them again and again. Pausing briefly to rail at the heavens for the terrible injustice of keeping the entire series out of the hands of pulp fans everywhere except for a grotesquely overpriced (and hideous) hardcover collection, I set to work on my story.

The universe of the Moon Man, the streets of Great City, provided endless inspiration. This is a character that reads like New Pulp right out of the gates. It's as if Davis had a crystal ball when he was crafting his gems and wrote the stories for today's audience. The world of the Moon Man was ever-changing, evolving and purists today who bemoan the added depth New Pulp writers are justly trying to bring to other classic pulp characters for modern readers would do well to observe that Davis pulled it off in spades back in the 1930s.

Crafting my tale was simplicity itself. The characters leapt off the page, the world was so unique and varied. Really, all I needed was a crackling plot, some action sequences and to place these in the incredible layered world Davis gave us with his stories.

Simple as that.

I couldn't resist having a little fun with the Argus glass helmet though thus the snowman gag and the pressed glass, heightened hearing scene. One thing lacking in the originals is the uses the glass dome can be put to.

The vertical auto park really did exist however it was in Chicago, not Great City. Stumbling across a photo of it online I knew that it had to go into a pulp tale. Luckily I hit on a newsreel showing it in action and the issue of Popular Science from the 1930s which provided the specifics for the thing.

It's my hope that this new collection of Moon Man stories, the first of its kind, will spur interest in not only the character but the original tales as well. There are still 19 original tales I'm dying to read. Come on Altus Press, what are you waiting for? And, if you've never read an original Moon Man tale, then buckle up, you're in for a wild ride. This anthology is only the beginning of your trip to the moon!

Google "lost classic pulp gem" and you'll get the Moon Man – one of the most original, entertaining and thought-provoking pulp characters to ever come down the pike. I hope you enjoyed the tales in this book and will come back for more.

ANDREW SALMON-is a two-time Pulp Factory Award nominee, and won the award for his first Sherlock Holmes story, "The Adventure of the Locked Room" (*Sherlock Holmes Consulting Detective: Volume One*). He is also a Pulp Ark Award nominee and has been nominated for an Arthur Ellis Award (the equivalent of the Edgar) in his native Canada. His work has appeared in numerous magazines, including *Masked Gun Mystery*, *Planetary Stories, Parsec, Storyteller, TBT* and *Thirteen Stories.*

He is creating a Brand/X superhero serial novel currently running in *A Thousand Faces Magazine.*

He has published or appeared in fourteen books: *The Forty Club* (which Midwest Book Reviews calls "a good solid little tale you will definitely carry with you for the rest of your life"), *The Light Of Men*, which has been called "a book of such immense significance that it is not only meant to be read, but also to be experienced... a work of grim power" – C. Saunders. *Secret Agent X: Volume One* and *Three, Ghost Squad: Rise of the Black Legion* (with Ron Fortier), *Jim Anthony Super Detective: Volume One, Sherlock Holmes Consulting Detective: Volumes One, Two and Three, Dan Fowler G-Man: Volume One, Black Bat Mystery: Volume One, Mars McCoy Space Ranger Volume One, The Dark Land* ("a straight out science-fiction thriller that fires on all cylinders" – Pulp Fiction Reviews) and *The Moon Man Volume One*, and *Mystery Men: Volume Two* (with Mark Halegua) constitute his work for Airship 27 to date.

Andrew's work will also appear in the upcoming Rick Ruby anthologies from Airship 27 as well as many other projects in various stages of development.

To learn more about his work check out the following links:
http://www.amazon.com/Andrew-Salmon/e/B002NS5KR0/ref=ntt_athr_dp_pel_pop_2.
www.airship27hangar.com
www.lulu.com/AndrewSalmon
www.lulu.com/thousand-faces

OUT OF BUSINESS
by
Gary Lovisi

*T*he place was full of people. A horde of male and female revelers jostling each other at the bar, busy celebrating the fact that Prohibition – the so-called "Noble Experiment" which had made all alcoholic beverages illegal and brought on a decade of violent gangsterism – had finally ended.

"Thank God and good riddance!" Ned Dargan sighed and took another drink. Not that Dargan, or any of the other patrons of The Easy Lady had ever obeyed that law. The bar had been a notorious speakeasy in the day, one of Great City's more well-trod attractions among the elite and even the more common folk. Of which Ned Dargan was definitely one of the most common.

The place was a huge establishment and it was owned by a fellow named Frankie Moran, a man said to be affiliated with the local Mafia hoodlums – but in the Irish wing. Still and all, he and his boys could be dangerous so it was wise for everyone there to watch their P's and Q's, and for the most part everyone did.

But things happen from time to time in a place like The Easy Lady when the booze flows too freely, sometimes blood flows too. It started when Ned Dargan saw some big goon of a lout manhandle a dame he'd taken a fancy to. He didn't like what he was seeing done by the guy and when he saw Charlotte trying to fight her masher off as he grabbed at her, he decided to get involved.

"Get yer grubby paws offa me!" little Charlotte screamed, striking the larger man with her tiny balled up fists. "I'm not yer plaything! Move off, buster!"

The man just laughed, Dargan could see he was mobbed up by the cut of his suit and the manner of his attitude; no dame was going to deny him. This was not the type of man to take no for an answer so he just grabbed the gal and crushed her lips to his own, in a hard wet kiss that ran over her face and then down her neck.

Ned Dargan had seen enough. While he knew little Charlotte could usually take care of herself, he couldn't help but step in to equal things a bit.

The masher, one of them flashy Eye-talian gangster types in an expensive sharkskin suit, stood easily six feet tall and had a hundred pounds on slim little Charlotte, fifty pounds on Dargan himself, so it was hardly a fair fight. But fighting was all Dargan knew, being an ex-pug he loved a good brawl.

Well, one was about to begin now. In fact, it would become a small war!

Dargan grabbed the Eye-talian and spun him around like a top, "Hey, bub, the dame said she doesn't appreciate none of your attentions. So blow!"

The guy shook off Dargan's hand, stepped back, looked the short, squat fighter squarely in the eyes and barked, "You know who I am!"

"Yeah, I know you're a moron who's bothering a dame I happen to fancy. Got it! Now blow, I say, or you'll get a knuckle sandwich in your big fat mouth."

The larger man grew hard, angry, looked at the shorter, squat, no-necked guy in front of him with disdain. "You don't know who you're messing with you ugly little troglodyte!"

"Trog – le – what!" Dargan barked angry, deeply insulted. He knew what the word meant and he didn't like it one bit, especially since it was a cruel but rather apt description of his physical appearance he had heard since he'd been a kid.

"I'm Antonio Strapolo, my brother runs this city, you damn potatohead!" Suddenly the hoodlum reached into his jacket for the gun that rested in the shoulder holster under his arm.

Dargan saw the move and reacted faster, out of sheer boxing instinct. He slapped the gun out of Strapolo's hand to fling it to the barroom floor where it went off with a resounding report that got everyone's attention.

Now the place was in utter pandemonium. Patrons suddenly cleared out of the way leaving plenty of room for the two men to solve their 'differences'. The bouncers, knowing a mobster was involved, stepped back and disappeared.

Once Strapolo boldly drew closer to strike the shorter man, Dargan gave the guy the knuckle sandwich he'd been asking for, with mustard and relish. The ex-pug balled his massive fist into a sledgehammer of pure power and force that plowed straight into the face of the gangster. One blow and Strapolo was knocked out stone cold to fall down to the floor in an undignified lump.

"I still got it, baby!" Dargan shouted to Charlotte glowing with pride. He hugged her to him. "Are you all right?"

"I'm fine, Ned, but you've gone and done it now! You've plastered one of the Strapolo brothers and they run this town, and this bar too, through my boss, Frankie Moran. You've really stepped into it," Charlotte said fearful for his future health.

Ned just smiled, "I'm not worried about him."

"Well, you should be, Ned," and she moved away from the ex-boxer as if he had suddenly contracted a deadly disease.

"Hah, don't worry none about me, doll, I been up against worst palookas than that guy before," Dargan insisted his gaze lost in Charlotte's deep blue eyes.

"Ned, look out!" Charlotte suddenly shouted. "Behind you!"

Dargan turned swiftly and saw three tough-looking men approaching.

"Move off, doll, looks like I got another bout coming up," Dargan placed Charlotte behind him out of danger, then he moved forward towards the three men who were now busy helping their fallen boss.

By now most of the bar patrons had moved off, many going outside on the sidewalk; those that remained inside were pinned up against the far walls in an effort to see the impending action without being in the line of fire. All watched in rapt fascination as the three gangsters helped Antonio Strapolo to his feet.

Dargan smiled, it was obvious the mob chief was still seeing stars and smarting from the blow to the head. It was good to know that his right still had some significant slam to it.

The three gangsters soon got their boss to his feet, revived him, and once he came to his senses, Strapolo pointed to Dargan and barked, "Kill him! Kill that bum now!"

"Sure thing, boss," a tall, slim gangster replied. "Come on, boys, let's show this little monkey the error of his ways and teach him a lesson."

Then they fanned out and approached Dargan. One slipping brass knuckles over the fingers of his right hand, one had a gun drawn holding it butt out, to use as a sap. Their leader drew a long, slim stiletto and he looked like he meant business.

Then the three men were on Ned Dargan and the melee began.

Three men on one was not fair but that didn't bother an ex-pug like Ned Dargan that much. He'd been in tougher scrapes before. He was used to hard-boiled brawling action, craved it even. Neither did it bother him that the three men were all bigger than he was, or that they were all dangerous gangsters, and all armed. Dargan was a former championship boxer, he knew the fight trade inside and out. He was always ready for a good scrap, and being lately retired from the ring because of a hand injury, he really missed the action.

So when Strapolo's three bodyguards moved in on Dargan to teach him a lesson – they were surprised when he attacked them like the rabid little bulldog he was – and taught them a lesson!

The tough little pug was in and among the three gangsters in a flash, before they even knew what was happening. He was jabbing like the old days warding off their blows, then coming in tight with sharp uppercuts plowing right under the chin, or hard haymakers to the side of the head that put the men down – one – two – three! Like a ton of bricks all three men went down in the matter of a single minute.

Ned Dargan thought he heard the bell, so he stopped the fight.

He looked at the three gangsters laying in a heap on the floor in front of him. He raised his arms in victory. "Them guys never knew what hit 'em! I still got it! I'm still the champ!" he shouted triumphantly.

Dargan saw that everyone was looking at him, some cheering, others clapping, others nervous, but he basked in the glow from Charlotte's pride for him. Then his eyes caught the dark hatred from the mobster whose men lay helpless on the floor.

Dargan heard the bell again.

Only this time he knew it wasn't a bell, it was a whistle and that meant a police raid was in progress. The bar was soon full of Great City coppers and at their head was the brash and grim Lieutenant Gil McEwan.

Dargan suddenly realized he had made a big mistake getting into a public brawl. Especially in a mob-run place. The ex-pug's thoughts now shifted to his friend and associate Steve Thatcher – the man who he, and only one other, knew was the notorious Moon Man. His rash actions tonight had put all the Moon Man's plans in dire peril.

"That's him, Lieutenant!" Antonio Strapolo shouted. "He attacked me, then attacked my men. Arrest him! Now!"

McEwan moved in and spoke to Antonio Strapolo as his men surrounded Dargan. Then the detective spoke to the three men who had been so obviously beaten as they got to their feet, then to Frankie Moran the owner of the place, and finally even to little Charlotte. McEwan shook his head, while he didn't like what he saw, the story he got from everyone was the same.

It meant bad news for the ex-pug.

McEwan nodded, his men moved in. Charlotte tried to explain Dargan's actions had been due to self-defense, but she shied away from explaining anything further and she did not mention Strapolo's men had been armed. In fact, no one in the bar even mentioned having seen a pair of brass knucks, or a gun, or even a stiletto in the hands of Strapolo's men.

McEwan saw to it that Dargan was cuffed and led out of the bar. "Being an ex-prizefighter, this can be serious if you used your fists on the men. And you sure enough did from the look of the damage you did here. All four of these men have been beaten pretty badly, and you without a nick or a scratch on you, excepting to your knuckles."

"It was self defense!" Dargan insisted.

"Looks like assault with a deadly weapon to me. Could get you prison time," McEwan explained as he led Dargan out of the bar. "Come along peacefully, or you'll get a shellacking from me boys in the van."

"What about the other guys?" Dargan asked.

"Appears to me you're the one who threw the beating, so you're the one we are arresting. The others can all go."

"Well, I'll be...!"

Ned Dargan shook his head but he went with the police and did as he was told. He walked off surrounded by a group of blue-coated uniformed policemen. Charlotte ran to him, hugged him, kissed him, thanked him, then whispered in his ear, "I'm sorry, I tried, but I couldn't speak the truth. You know how it is here."

"I know it, and it's all right, doll," Dargan told her softly. He didn't want Charlotte to get in trouble by speaking up for him, but he was disappointed nevertheless that she had not done so.

"I'm sorry, Ned," she cried.

"Listen, doll, do me a favor? Get word to Steve Thatcher if you can, tell him I'm in lockup."

"Sure thing, Ned, I'll try to get word to him."

The next morning Great City police detective, Stephen Thatcher got the news of Ned Dargan's arrest even before little Charlotte could tell him. He got it direct from Lieutenant McEwan himself.

"So, I heard you had a wild situation last night?" Thatcher asked.

Gil McEwan was Thatcher's best friend and a tried and true copper. He was also obsessive in his hunt for the notorious master criminal known

"Get word to Steve Thatcher if you can."

as the Moon Man – whose secret identity was that of Steve Thatcher. To complicate matters, Steve's gal, Sue, was McEwan's daughter.

"By damn, I did! We got a call to The Easy Lady, that old mob speakeasy out on 4th where some ex-pug broke up the place in a wild battle with local hoods. Not a good idea, I'd be thinking generally, but it turns out this one guy put all four of them down hard and fast. What a brawl! I heard it was a beautiful thing."

"Really?" Thatcher asked, learning the fellow had been an ex-pug got him thinking. Could it be his friend and agent Ned Dargan, who went by the code name of "Angel"?

"Yep," McEwan continued, "he went on a wild tear, used his fists like hammers on four guys, and these weren't just any old guys either, it was Antonio Strapolo and three of his goons. Well, let me tell you, by the looks of things when I got there, the gangsters sure got the worst of that 'discussion'. I felt kinda sorry for the pug, though, since he was the last man standing and a boxer who had used his fists, I had to take him in. Those fists are considered deadly weapons, so it was assault with a deadly weapon plain as day."

Thatcher shrugged, "So he beat up some crummy mobsters, they probably deserved it," Thatcher said carefully, thinking it through as to what effect this might have on his actions as the Moon Man. "Especially if it was those Strapolo boys. Couldn't you cut the guy some slack? Let him off with a warning?"

"No way. I mean, I woulda liked to let him go, Steve, but Strapolo insisted and pressed charges, and by the looks of him and his men, the fighter went way over the line on this. I had no choice but to bring him in."

"That could get him prison time," Thatcher said careful not to allow his deep concern for his friend and associate to show. By now he figured the man in question had to be Ned Dargan, aka Angel. And that posed some problems. If Angel was locked up, that meant the Moon Man's program to steal from the rich to aid the needy and poor of Great City was effectively stymied because Angel was the one person who gave out the stolen funds to the needy This could put the Moon Man out of business!

"Did you get a name on this guy?"

"Yeah, an ex-pug by the name of Ned Dargan," McEwan said, shaking his head in consternation. "No record, leastways nothing serious, but he busted up four guys pretty bad. It's for the judge to decide now, but he'll stay in lockup until the case goes to trial, or he gets a good enough lawyer to get him out on bail. You know him?"

"No," Thatcher lied convincingly, "but I saw him fight a few times, years back. He was good."

"By damn, I wish I'd gotten there earlier and seen the brawl since the beginning. I only saw the aftermath. Witnesses said he put them hoods down one – two – three!"

"So what will happen to him now?"

"Like I say, he's got no record, so he might make bail if he gets a good enough lawyer – which I doubt. He's not one flush for cash. He'll probably lay in city jail until the judge gets the case. Then it's bye-bye and prison for old Ned. Assault with a deadly weapon, Steve. That's a serious offense in this town."

"I know," Thatcher said thoughtfully. How was he ever going to get Angel out of this mess?

"You should know, Steve," McEwan added, "it's your own father as police chief who has made sure that we enforce these laws to the letter."

"I know," Thatcher repeated gloomily. All he could think of now was poor Ned, alone in a jail cell, with a prison rap breathing down his neck. How could he make this all go away?

Could the Moon Man do something?

The problem was that with Ned – Angel – in jail, who would give out the money the Moon Man 'collected' that was a lifeline to the poor of Great City? That was Angel's job; he was known to the people in need and trusted by them. There was no one else Thatcher could use.

Steve Thatcher considered doing it himself – but it would be just too risky and would link him too closely with the Moon Man – who was still wanted for a murder he did not commit. Thatcher was also a police detective, so he had to walk a delicate tightrope with his Moon Man activities not to give away his true identity.

There was only one other person Thatcher could trust. That was Sue, lovely Sue, his girl. She was the only other person, beside Angel, who knew Steve was the Moon Man, but he could never place the woman he loved in such a dangerous position. Thatcher just couldn't involve Sue on this. He would not place her at risk for any reason. No, he just had to find some way to clear Ned. And do it soon!

Steve Thatcher suddenly realized that his life had become a lot more complicated. He looked at Gil McEwan, smiled, "Well, Gil, it looks like you made a good arrest, so congratulations are in order. But you know, I'm going over to the jail to see this Dargan fellow. Just to get his side of the story."

"What do you mean?" McEwan asked suspiciously.

"I mean, he beat up Antonio Strapolo and three of his goons. I don't think I like that kind of organized gangsterism making its way into Great City."

McEwan thought this over for a moment.

"By damn, I guess you're right, Steve," McEwan admitted. He didn't like hoodlums either and if they were making inroads into his city that was bad news. "Until now the presence of the Mafia has been limited here, with Strapolo that may mean they're expanding their operations."

"My thoughts exactly," Thatcher added.

"Good looking out, I'll alert your father. As chief he'll want to be kept up-to-date on any developments. Go see Dargan, see what he knows about this."

"I will," Thatcher said and was off.

The cell was small and cold. The ex-pug was alone. He'd only had a few drinks at The Easy Lady, not enough to get him drunk, but the alcohol had obviously impaired his judgment. Dargan realized he'd made a serious error by engaging in a brawl in a public place. And with four mob guys! He should have taken the action outside, away from any crowd and the cops.

"I must be crazy!" he whispered to himself, but even allowing the booze had impaired his judgment, Dargan still couldn't countenance that Eye-talian gorilla glomming onto his gal, Charlotte. Even though, officially, Charlotte was not really his gal.

Furthermore, Dargan had truly enjoyed the melee, it was like being back in the ring again, like old times – having four bouts on his card and winning all four by KO's! But he'd made a grievous mistake by his rash action and it now placed the Moon Man in a troublesome dilemma. For with "Angel" locked away here in jail and out of action – perhaps to go to prison – who would distribute the Moon Man's loot to the needy and poor?

Dargan sighed deeply, sad he had disappointed his friend. He knew the sole reason Steve Thatcher had become the Moon Man was to take money from the rich to help the poor of his city. It was a noble – though criminal – enterprise. The Moon Man was like a modern day Robin Hood and now Ned realized he might have put an end to all that good work.

"I really messed up," Dargan muttered softly to himself.

"That you did, my friend," a voice suddenly answered him. Dargan quickly looked up to see the smiling face of Steve Thatcher on the other side of the bars of his cell.

"Hi, Boss."

"Hi, Angel."

There was no one else in the small cell block, no guards present, no other prisoners. Thatcher took out the key to unlock the cell and enter. The two men shook hands and clasped shoulders. They were long-time friends and Dargan idolized Thatcher and his work.

"I'm sorry, Boss," Dargan said, when the two men were sitting upon his cot alone.

"Tell me all of it, Angel. What happened?"

Dargan related the entire tale about the man bothering Charlotte, the fights and his arrest by McEwan.

"Strapolo and the mob complicates things," Thatcher said carefully, "but then again, perhaps things can be bent to our advantage?"

"How so, Boss?"

"I'll have to look into this a bit more deeply. Right now I have to get you a good lawyer and get you out of here on bail, if I can. I also want to speak to your gal, Charlotte, see what she can tell me. Maybe brace Strapolo, see if I can get him to be reasonable and drop the charges."

"He's not the reasonable type, Boss."

"We'll see."

"That'll never happen. He's got it in for me because of Charlotte," Dargan warned.

"Perhaps a visit from the Moon Man will change his attitude?"

Ned Dargan smiled at that, "Be careful with them people, Boss."

"I will, and I'll get you out of here, Angel. By hook or by crook, I'll get you out of here – or the Moon Man is effectively out of business."

Steve Thatcher drove his sleek black roadster out to the Huntington section of Great City. It was an area of big homes and large walled properties where the wealthy – famous and infamous – lived. It was the place where at Number 142, Antonio Strapolo had his home.

Strapolo was the younger brother of mob kingpin Victor Strapolo. He dabbled in the rackets but had never really been a major player like his older brother, but because of that connection he held some serious juice. This younger Strapolo spent all his time going to nightclubs, fooling with party girls and drinking and gambling too much. Steve Thatcher knew all this and he knew that the best way to make Strapolo drop the charges against Dargan was to do to this mobster what the mob so often did to witnesses against them – intimidation. And the perfect agency for intimidation – even to intimidate a Mafia gangster – was the Moon Man!

The house was dark as Thatcher pulled up his roadster and parked it down the street around the corner. Thatcher was dressed all in black and quickly took out the case from his trunk. This held the costume of the dreaded Moon Man. He carried the case towards the house and entered through an upstairs window, finding the place dark and seemingly empty. It was late.

Thatcher found himself in a bedroom. He knew the layout; he was directly across the hall from Strapolo's bedroom, now he immediately began to transform himself into the Moon Man.

Thatcher quickly donned the black cloak that covered his clothing, put on the black gloves, and then took out the twin halves that formed the mysterious Argus globe. This light-weight, fishbowl-like glass globe he deftly fit over his head, making himself into an eerie and mysterious figure. No one could see into the smooth mirror-like sphere to determine his identity but he could see out of it as clear as day, even in the darkness of night. Lastly he took out the .45 to complete his ensemble, and became the feared notorious criminal, the Moon Man.

Now Steve Thatcher was ready to make his play and to instill some terror into Antonio Strapolo and hopefully save Ned Dargan from prison.

The second floor of the big house was quiet as the Moon Man exited the empty room across the hall from where the mobster was sleeping. The intruder moved across the hall to Strapolo's bedroom door standing boldly in the open hallway as he carefully reached for the doorknob. At that moment two of Strapolo's goons entered the hallway from the far end. They took one look at the strange figure and shouted in awe and fear.

"What the heck is that!" one blurted in surprise.

"It's him! It's the Moon Man! He's a wanted man! Blast him!"

But the Moon Man was quicker, already aiming his .45 at the two mobsters even as they tried to draw their guns.

"Put down your weapons and you will not be hurt!" an eerie voice warned the men from behind the round sphere atop the super criminal's head.

The two mob goons looked at each other curiously, then grinned evilly.

"Nix on that! We take him now!" one of the gangsters shouted going for his gun, as his companion did likewise.

The Moon Man had to act fast and now had no choice. With pinpoint precision, he let loose two rounds from his .45 that penetrated the chests of each of the two men, dropping them to the floor before either of them could get off a shot.

"Not much time now," Thatcher muttered to himself, sorry the situation had given him no choice in shooting the thug guards. He quickly checked to see that both men were out of commission, knowing that the discharge of his weapon would soon alert the entire household. Strapolo probably had more guards; they'd be coming here soon to see what had happened, so he had to act fast.

The Moon Man crossed the hall and quickly entered the bedroom of Antonio Strapolo. The mobster was already awake from the noise, but obviously disoriented from sleeping off a night of heavy boozing; he was sitting up in bed rubbing the sleep from his eyes when those eyes beheld the most amazing and uncanny sight he'd ever scene before in his life.

"You, the Moon Man? Here?" he stammered, fear growing within him as he beheld the macabre image in the half-light of his darkened bedroom.

Thatcher did not answer but quickly grabbed the gangster and roughly pulled him out of his bed, holding him hard up against the wall with one black-gloved hand around his throat, as the other hand pointed the cold steel of a .45 into the man's trembling face.

"We are criminals, you and I. You understand that?" the eerie voice growled from behind the mirror-like glass worn upon the head of his bizarre intruder.

Strapolo stood frozen in terror as his eyes stared at the weird thing that held him captive.

Was this a hit!

Where were his men?

"Answer me!" the voice behind the Argus globe barked in rage.

"Yes, I understand," Strapolo replied frantically.

"We do not step on each others turf. Do you understand?"

"Yes! Yes, of course. Please? What do you want?"

"Drop your charges against Ned Dargan, or I can promise you, you will never live to see your next birthday," the mysterious voice threatened from behind the shiny glass helmet. Strapolo tried to look into that mirror-like glass to see if he could determine the identity of his attacker, but it was useless. He could see nothing, and that fact made him more nervous.

"Is this a hit?" Strapolo asked in terror.

"It could be. Do you want it to be?" the grim voice taunted.

Antonio Strapolo started to tremble in terror. His birthday was next week. This monster that held him helpless was telling him that he would not live out the week unless he dropped the charges against that Dargan man. The hoodlum had to think fast to find a way out of this. Save his life.

"Ah, I see it now! So he's your man?" Strapolo asked.

"No, you are wrong, he is nobody, but he was protecting a girl I know, so I figure I owe him. What you should know is that the police of this city are aware of your brother's plans to expand the Mafia here. So if you drop the charges on this man a court case that will involve you – and him – will never see the light of day. Inconvenient questions need never be asked – or answered. It will be good for all concerned," the Moon Man explained quickly.

"And what about you? What do you get?"

"Money. That is all I'm after. You know what they say in the newspapers about me. All I want is a small payment for my involvement. Drop the charges against Dargan, then give him $10,000 in cash to pay me for my service. That will satisfy me."

"And what if I say no?" Strapolo said carefully, paying the cash was no problem but he was thinking it through, looking for some way out.

"Then I splatter your brains all over this nice bed," the Moon Man growled, thinking quick. He hadn't wanted to kill the two guards – he had warned them and it had been done in self defense – but their deaths might prove useful now. "Look outside your room after I leave, you'll find your two friends, dead. Then see if I don't mean business! Be smart and drop the charges – or be stupid and dead – in which case the charges will be dropped anyway because you'll be gone and won't be able to testify. It makes no difference to me what you decide - but do it quickly."

Strapolo shivered, starring in terror at his trembling visage reflected back at him in the mirror-globe helmet of the creature in front of him, "All right, I'll do it, I agree."

"Do not betray me. Your birthday is coming soon and it would be a pity for you to miss it."

Strapolo swallowed hard.

"Just let me go. I promise I'll do as you say."

The Moon Man eased his hand from the throat of Antonio Strapolo and then slugged him in the head with the butt of his .45, rendering the man unconscious. Then he immediately exited Strapolo's bedroom, reentering the empty room across the hall where he had left his case. The house was still quiet, the two goons still lying peacefully dead on the floor at the other end of the hall. For how long things would remain that way was anyone's guess. He had to move fast.

Quickly Thatcher took off his Moon Man garb, placing the two halves of the Argus globe into the case; along with the black cloak, gloves and his .45. Then he nimbly exited the room through the open window he had come in through, crawled down the trellis to the ground below, and was gone. He was in his roadster and driving away a moment later. The entire operation had taken less than five minutes.

"I can't believe it, Boss!" Ned Dargan said, elated that he was free. The two men were meeting at the old abandoned warehouse which was one of the places they used for their secret operations.

"I'm glad you're finally back, Angel," Steve Thatcher said with a grin.

"Let me tell you, Strapolo not only dropped the charges, he gave me this envelope. He still looked scared and shaky. The envelope was stuffed with cash. I counted ten thousand dollars!" Dargan said with a grim smile. "Seems the Moon Man had something to do with this, if I'm not mistaken."

"Could be," Thatcher laughed.

"Well, thanks, Boss. You pulled me out of a tight spot," Dargan's appreciation glowing from his tough scared face.

"Well, just don't get in any other scrapes, all right? McEwan will be watching you, so become invisible, and stay away from that bar and that gal, Charlotte. In the meantime, I know of some people in the slums out by the old Maguire Mill that could sure use some extra cash to pay their bills. See to it, will you, Angel."

"Sure thing, Boss, I'm just glad Angel and the Moon Man are back in business."

"Me too, Angel, me too."

THE END

PHASES OF THE MOON MAN
Part Two

*I*n "Out of Business" I took a bit of a different tack, this time concentrating on one of the lesser – but essential – characters in the saga, the colorful ex-boxer, Ned Dargan. Ned's valiant protection of a mob dame he has taken a fancy to, and his short temper, end up placing the Moon Man in a dire situation that must be solved – and the Moon Man solves it admirably. At least I hope you think so. In the end, it is up to you, the reader and fan, whether I have done my job successfully, but I can tell you one thing: I loved writing these stories. I hope that comes through when you read them. They were great pulp crime fun to recreate; I love the characters and the relationships between them. It's an amazing saga and I have to tell you that I am not just a writer of these two tales, I'm a pulp fan and reader myself: a person who loves the heroes presented to us in the classic pulps, and the pulp paperbacks. It has been a real privilege for me to continue the crime adventures of this unique pulp hero. I want to thank Ron Fortier and the kind people at Airship27 who made it all possible. I hope you enjoy my two contributions to the Moon Man saga and hope some day to add once again to the pulp adventures of the Argus-globed hero.

GARY LOVISI - has been a writer for many years of all kinds of fiction and non-fiction. That fiction includes hard crime stories and novels, science fiction, horror and even westerns. his story "Lead Poisoning" just came out in the new western noir anthology *On Dangerous Ground* (Cemetery Dance, 2011), while under his own Gryphon Books imprint he edited the hard crime magazine, *Hardboiled* – which won a Western

Writers of America SPUR Award last year for publishing the Best Western Short Story of 2010 – a hard-boiled western story. He is also a Mystery Writers of America, Edgar Award nominee.

In his non-fiction he has written many articles on books and book collecting for various magazines, as well as editing his own book collectors magazine, Paperback Parade for over 20 years. He sponsors an annual book show in New York City that is now in its 24th year.

He has another book from Airship27 out now; an original Sherlock Holmes crime novel, *The Baron's Revenge*. It really kicks and loyal Holmes fans should look for it.

His most recent books include *Ultra-Boiled* (Ramble House, hardcover and trade paperback, www.ramblehouse.com) a collection of 23 of his hardest crime and noir short stories. *Bad Girls Need Love Too* (Krause, www.krausebooks.com), a wonderful hardcover compilation of classic pulp paperback cover art showcasing salty dames, bad girls, and wild sexy situations in cover art; also including the saucy, often outrageous and provocative blurbs used to sell these books. He recently did three trade paperback books for Borgo Press / Wildside Press in their new "Doubles" series. These books include *Murder of A Bookman*, a Bentley Hollow biblio-mystery; *Driving Hell's Highway*, a man with no past and no future travels the dark highways of America in this violent surreal noir; and *Gargoyle Nights*, his homage to the fantastical horror of H.P. Lovecraft and Clark Ashton Smith. If you would like to find out more about these books or any of his other work, please go to: www.gryphonbooks.com

THE ROBIN HOOD OF
THE PULPS

Of all the colorful and bizarre crime fighting heroes of the pulp magazines, none was more so than the Moon Man who appeared regularly in the pages of *10 DETCTIVE ACES*.

At the height of the Great Depression, the fictional metropolis of Great City, like most of America, had come face to face with an impoverished populace. Lost and forgotten souls living in shanty towns and filling the soup and bread lines that sprang up at local churches. The masses were looking for a hand out and a hand up out of these dire times. Yet while thousands suffered and went hungry, a select few of the elite wealthy class continued to thrive and live their obscene, extravagant lifestyles. It was a moral injustice flaunted publicly and no one seemed to be able to do anything about. Not until the coming of the Moon Man.

Police Detective Sgt. Stephen Thatcher, only son of the Police Chief, could not reconcile what he saw every day on the streets of Great City. It haunted his nights so badly that recalling the exploits of the famous thief of Nothingham Forest, he made the decision to become a modern day Robin Hood. To that end he devised a truly fantastic disguise using a mysterious compound known as Argus glass. It was an early version of the one way mirror, shaped in the form of a round globe and worn over his head. Once in place, Steve could see out, but others could not see through the silver sheen of the outer surface. Steve built a special deflector type apparatus within the sphere that prevented his breath from fogging up the glass. To accompany this strange glass helmet, Thatcher donned a high color black cloak with several hidden pockets to hold his pistols and matching black gloves. So dark was the get-up that when he was first spotted moving through the night, only the shiny globe was visible to viewers and it appeared like a miniature moon floating in the air. Thus he was soon labeled by witnesses, and ultimately the press, as the Moon Man.

Now, the Moon Man only stole from the very rich, people who would not in the slightest be hurt by the lost monies, jewels or furs he absconded with. The proceeds of these daring thefts were secretly donated to various churches and charities throughout Great City with anonymous instructions that they were to help the poor and down-trodden. Since much of this was delicate and time-consuming work, Thatcher took a big gamble and recruited an ally to help him dispense of the Moon Man's loot. That ally was a tough as nails ex-boxer named Ned "Angel" Dargan. Angel was short and squat, with at twisted nose, from too many breaks, and cauliflower ears. A bad injury to one of his arms ended his fighting career and Angel would have become just another of the faceless lost souls of Great City had he not been befriended by the young, rookie police sergeant.

Angel owed his friend his very life and was completely loyal to the Moon Man. Not only did he enjoy his role in delivering the stolen funds to the needy but on many occasions his bravery and fighting tenacity saved the Moon Man from certain capture or worse.

But the burly ex-pugilist wasn't the Moon Man's only aide. Early on in his fledgling criminal career, Steve found it necessary to confide in his fiancée, the beautiful and smart Sue McEwen. This was an extremely ticklish situation, as Sue was the only child of the city's finest man-hunter, Chief of Detectives Gil McEwen, the very man who had sworn an oath to capture the Moon Man and bring him to justice. Sue was twenty-two, a tough cookie with a shrewd mind and was ever resourceful in helping her beloved evade the long arm of the law. She also carried a small pearl handled automatic and was a crack shot thanks to her father's instructions.

The creative genius behind this series was writer Frederick C. Davis. Davis was also known as the writer of the first twenty novels starring another popular pulp hero,Operator 5, writing as Curtis Steele. Davis began his writing career while in college in the 1920s, writing and selling a story a week to the then burgeoning pulps. They paid for his education and quickly established him as a dependable wordsmith editor's could rely on. By the 1930s, he had established a routine of writing from nine o'clock in the morning until four o'clock in the afternoon, six days a week. His daily output was thirty completed double spaced pages, or, 125,000 words a month. For nearly ten years prior to World War II, he wrote a million words a year.

There were 38 Moon Man stories between June 1933 to January 1937. All of these stories have been collected in two hardbacks. "The Night

Nemesis", The Complete Adventures of the Moon Man – Volume One edited by Garyn G. Roberts and Gary Hoppenstand and published by The Purple Prose Press, Bowling Green, Ohio and "The Silver Spectre", The Complete Adventures of the Moon Man – Volume Two, compiled and edited by Robert Weinberg, The Battered Silicon Dispatch Box.

So strong is the appeal of this uniquely pulp hero that to this day new writers find it impossible to resist adding new exploits to his saga such as the five marvelous tales offered in this collection. These talented new pulp writers have devoted themselves to keeping the legend of this modern day Robin Hood and alive and well; much to all our pleasure. Rest assured there will be many more volumes in this series devoted to one of pulpdom's most bizarre heroes.

Ron Fortier
Fort Collins, CO
2/2/2012
(Airship27@comcast.net)
(www.Airship27.com)

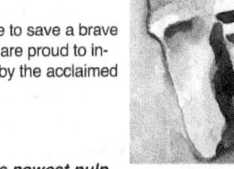

The Return of Baron Gruner

In 1902 Sir James Damery enlisted the aid of Sherlock Holmes to prevent the daughter of an old friend from marrying a womanizing Austrian named Adelbert Gruner who was suspected of murdering his first wife. Dr. Watson chronicled the case as "The Adventure of the Illustrious Client." By its conclusion, Gruner's evil intent was exposed to the young lady when Holmes came into possession of an album listing his many amorous conquests. A former prostitute mistress of the Baron's then took her own revenge by throwing acid in his face – permanently disfiguring him.

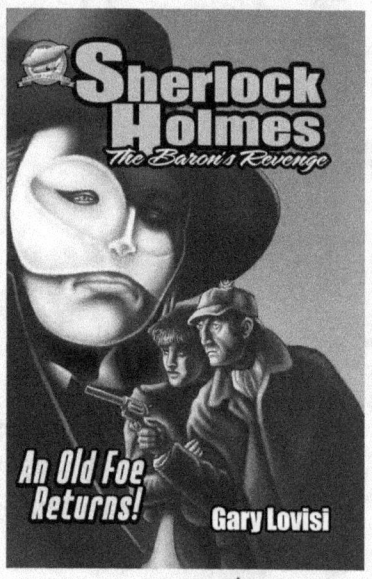

Holmes believed the matter concluded. He is proven wrong when a hideous murder occurs rife with evidence indicating the Baron has returned. Soon the Great Detective will learn he has been targeted for revenge in a cruel and sadistic fashion. Not only does the Baron wish his death but he is obsessed with causing Holmes emotional suffering. He desires nothing less that the complete and utter destruction of the Great Detective in body and soul.

Gary Lovisi spins a fast paced tale of horror and intrigue that is both suspenseful and poignant, all the while remaining true to Arthur Conan Doyle's original stories. "The Baron's Revenge" is a thrilling sequel to a classic Holmes adventure fans will soon be applauding.